Snowed in with the Mafia

Snowed In Series

Can be read in any order

Maya Black

This is a work of fiction. Names, characters, businesses, places, events and incidents are either the products of the author's imagination or used in a fictitious manner. Any resemblance to actual persons, living or dead, or actual events is purely coincidental.

Copyright © 2024 by Maya Black

All rights reserved.

No part of this book may be reproduced in any form or by any electronic or mechanical means, including information storage and retrieval systems, without written permission from the publisher, except for the use of brief quotations in a book review.

If you would like to use material from this book, prior written permission must be obtained by contacting the publisher at:

authormayablack@gmail.com

First edition: December 2024

Contents

Chapter 1	1
Chapter 2	5
Chapter 3	17
Chapter 4	27
Chapter 5	33
Chapter 6	41
Chapter 7	47
Chapter 8	59
Chapter 9	63
Chapter 10	69
Chapter 11	77
Chapter 12	85
Chapter 13	91
Chapter 14	95
Chapter 15	103
Chapter 16	111
Chapter 17	119
Chapter 18	129
Chapter 19	133
Chapter 20	139
Chapter 21	147
Chapter 22	155
Chapter 23	157
Chapter 24	163
Chapter 25	165
Chapter 26	169
Join Maya Black's Newsletter	175
About Maya Black	177
Also by Maya Black	179

Billy

My cock jerked as the words left my mouth and I gave the order for Melissa to do what I wanted. I surely hadn't intended the evening to wind up with me ordering my girl to show me her virgin cunt, but I'd given her the chance to say no.

I wouldn't have liked hearing it, but I would have honored her preferences.

She didn't do what I said immediately. Instead, my darling Melissa stood, her hands visibly quivering as she twisted them in the material of her blouse and approached closer.

I hummed in satisfaction; not even upset she wasn't obeying me promptly. I bent my finger toward her, and she came forward another step. Then one more, until she was standing straight in front of me and the delicious aroma of her innocence filled my nostrils.

She lifted her hand, and I tensed when she placed the tips of her fingers on the center of my chest. Melissa trailed them down, and my abdomen constricted. She let out a gentle breath and slid her fingers over my side, her delicate nails scratching gently over the fabric.

I'd never felt such tremendous fucking pleasure, and she wasn't even touching my bare skin. And for just a second, my eyes closed as I gave in to the sensations.

That's all the time my tiny wildcat needed.

She grabbed my gun and stumbled back.

I didn't rush her, didn't even move. I squinted my eyes and snarled low as she pointed the handgun squarely at me.

Her hands trembled and her expression expressed so much uncertainty.

My cock thickened even more.

I took a step forward, and she shook her head vehemently, moving to the side and away from the bed.

She was rushing toward the bedroom door, but my sweet child wouldn't get far even if she got out. The door stopped her from going any further, and I advanced, my movements languid, lazy even.

Melissa lifted her arms and clasped her fists securely around the weapon. The gun was now level with my chest.

"Don't come any closer or I'll shoot." Her voice shook as much as her hands did. "I swear to fucking God, Billy, I'll put a bullet right through your heart."

I grinned and reached down, squeezing the gigantic erection I had. It was growing thicker and harder with each passing second.

God she is fucking hot!

I moved forward until I crowded her. The muzzle of the gun now pressed to the center of my chest. I placed one hand beside her head on the door and used my other to curl my fingers around hers, keeping the gun pressed against my body.

She licked her lips, and I fixed my focus on the act, keeping back my groan at the vision of those gorgeous, pink and plump lips wrapped around my cock.

"Caught you off guard," she muttered. "Only reason I got this damn thing." Her voice was a little stronger, a little deeper. Her arousal was coming through.

I groaned at the very thought of her pussy being wet for me, all juicy and ripe for my cock. I leaned forward so the gun jabbed harder into my chest.

Her eyes widened as she glanced down, the worry on her expression apparent enough that I realized she had no plans of shooting me. "You surprised me, you sexy, little vixen." I grinned. "Bet your gorgeous ass has never even shot a gun, let alone held one."

She swung her gaze up to mine before it narrowed slightly. "You don't know shit about me."

Oh, how wrong she was.

"You know that's a lie, Sunshine."

She wet her lips once more. "I've held plenty of guns. You have to know how to conduct yourself when you're nothing and—"

I had a hold of her throat before she even finished getting the words out, my mouth so close to hers that I knew she'd feel my lips move as I spoke. "Never, ever fucking say you're nothing. And certainly not in my fucking presence, Sunshine."

I felt her hold on the gun lessen and, with a twist of my hand, snatched the gun away and held it up between us.

She stared at me, scared, and I couldn't help but breathe out in arousal.

"You've never fucking held a gun in your life." I switched the safety off to illustrate my point.

Her lips pushed together tightly, and I dragged my tongue across them, causing her to cry out in outrage and need.

With the safety still off, I retreated an inch and, while retaining her eyes, trailed my tongue up the barrel and licked the muzzle.

I placed the safety back in place and shoved the gun in the rear waistband of my sweats. And then, I slammed my hand on the door on the other side of her head and crowded the hell out of her.

"Now, lie to me again and tell me your pussy isn't wet right now."

Melissa

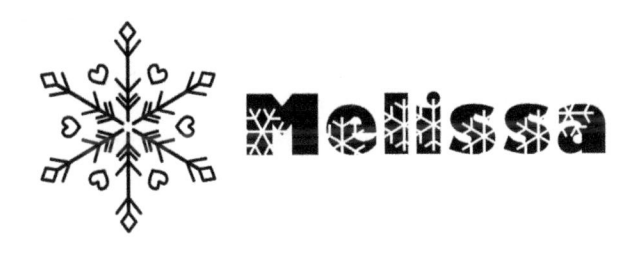

My heart was hammering. My body was hot in the most uncomfortable, exciting, way. I'd never been so scared, never genuinely feared for my life, but right now, I felt like I was being carried to my death by the huge beast of a man in front of me.

But even if I was afraid as hell right now, I knew what I was doing was right.

Because it would save my piece of shit brother and father. I shouldn't care what happened to them. It wasn't like they had ever done anything but bring my life turmoil and required me to bail them out more times than not.

But they're family.

The only ones I have left on this horrible planet.

And so, I proceeded further into the bowels of a disused warehouse that smelled like mold, age, and hints of decay, all in hopes I could trade for my family's lives with one of the largest drug lords in Desolation, New York.

Billy Leonard.

Smoothing my hands down the too tight shirt and short skirt, I felt stupid. But I needed to show Billy what I provided.

It wasn't money.

And it wasn't because I had any relationships that would help him.

It was my body and the use of it.

The only thing I had.

Maya Black

I swallowed forcefully, feeling even more silly at the concept that a man like Billy would make any kind of deal with me, let alone a sexual one that would get my father and brother out of the hole they'd dug themselves in.

A little later, the man brought me into a room that appeared like it had formerly been an office. A damaged, metal table was off to one side and a tan, slightly corroded filing cabinet on the other.

The walls were composed of white, peeling cinder block, and the aroma enveloping me was a mixture of stale air and disuse.

The big man didn't speak to me when he left me in the room.

I paced the length, my nervousness growing as the seconds passed by. Several times, I glanced at the door, and the more I was locked in here waiting for Billy to arrive, the more I told myself this was a stupid idea.

I had to get out of here.

I was in front of the door and grasping the handle before the thought had left my head, and just as I pulled it open, prepared to step out, my body met with one that was massive and hard and smelled like spicy, expensive cologne.

My hands automatically went to the strong chest, and my face smacked against layers of clothing. The suit under my palms wasn't able to hide the steady, unbothered beat of a heart.

Massive, tattooed hands reached up and seized my wrists. It wasn't unpleasant, but he applied purposeful pressure to let me know he could snap the bones as easily as tearing a turkey wishbone in half.

"I didn't order entertainment," the deep, extremely male voice replied with evident disinterest.

I tipped my head back… and back… until I was peering into the face of the crime lord himself, Billy Leonard.

I wanted to tell him I wasn't the fucking entertainment,

but I corrected myself instantly since that's exactly why the hell I was here.

God, he was dangerously attractive with short dark hair done a touch recklessly, strands flopping across his forehead, and piercing gray eyes that reminded me of stormy days.

I tugged my hands free and when he let me go, I knew it was because he allowed it.

Billy stood in the doorway, the three-piece suit he wore not masking his raw force and powerful build.

"Going somewhere?" he asked and stepped inside, pushing me backwards.

I saw the bodyguard right on the other side, and without glancing inside the room, he slammed the door, locking me in with a man I knew could kill me and bury my body where no one could find me.

I grasped the strap of my counterfeit purse but didn't walk any closer. I lingered beside the already closed door as if it would protect me. A moment passed with neither of us speaking, but I was vividly aware of the way Billy observed me with a stony face.

Dead eyes. That's what he had.

He headed toward the desk off to the side, the metal one that looked worse for wear. The piece of furniture was dented and scuffed with a stack of papers that had a covering of dust atop them. He leaned against the edge, arms folded, biceps bulging underneath his suit.

He looked deadly.

Violent.

He appeared obviously handsome in the way the devil was gorgeous but oozed pure wickedness.

"What is it you want?" His tone showed no inclination, his expression still voids of emotion.

It was evident he couldn't care less about my presence, and I now felt immensely silly for believing I could sway a criminal lord like Billy Leonard into achieving what I needed.

But I was here.

The worst thing he could tell me was to get the fuck out. Or maybe that wasn't the worst but that's the only route I was willing to think about.

My mouth felt dry, so trying to form any words was impossible. Finally, after telling myself to woman-the-fuck-up, I cleared my throat and shuffled on my feet. "I have a proposition for you."

He lifted a dark brow. He looked me up and down with the most unimpressed face a human could imagine.

"My brother and father…" I moistened my lips, my throat felt tight and dry. "They've gotten themselves into some trouble with you."

He still exhibited no reaction and didn't break eye contact.

I did everything in my ability to maintain my concentration on him. I knew it would come across as a weakness if I didn't. The last thing I wanted was to exhibit that in front of this man.

I liked to tell myself I was actually doing this because they were my only remaining relatives. But the truth was, my hand was being guided in this decision. If I didn't come up with the money to bail them out, no amount of running, or hiding would save me.

"I know who owes me money, Miss Barry."

My heart labored overtime. I didn't know why I was so taken aback by the fact he clearly knew who my brother and father were.

Duh!

Of course, he'd know all his business dealings. He wouldn't be as high on the food chain if he didn't.

"You know my name." I didn't phrase it like a question, and the little lift of his mouth wasn't at all humorous.

"Of course." He pushed away from the desk and stalked toward me. "I need to know all the lifelines of the pieces of shit who owe me, so that if need be, I know where to take lives."

I realized I'd been backing up as he drew closer, so now the cold, cinder brick wall halted my escape.

"I know everything about you, Melissa Barry." His voice had lowered deeper. "I knew you were asking around about me and trying to find me. You think I give my location out to anybody who comes knocking?"

He ran his thumb over his bottom lip, then sucked in his teeth as if the very thought annoyed him. "Such a pretty, little thing you are. I could eat you before you even realized it."

His voice was low, menacing. I couldn't comprehend him, his voice deep and dark, his pronunciation of Melissa immaculate and beautiful even yet he seemed so evil.

"I feel starved." His eyes slid to my lips. "How the fuck do you think you got this meeting with me? You think I didn't make sure I had every single minute of you here planned before I sent word out to have men bring you to me?"

Oh, God, I made a terrible mistake.

My heart was thumping so fiercely it hurt, the pain unlike anything I'd ever felt before.

It was terrifying.

Real, bone- deep fear that held me immobilized.

I felt that I had held the cards at this meeting, and had the upper hand. How incorrect I'd been.

"Your douchebag father owes me fifty grand, and that's increasing daily with interest." His voice fell even lower.

It was a tone I was sure he saved for individuals he was ready to strangle.

My throat pinched tighter.

God, I didn't know it was that much.

"And your brother, the dickless motherfucker who's not only a user, but also peddling his inferior quality, made-in-the-bathroom shit in my territory owes me twenty grand in potentially lost revenue."

I put my palms flat against the stone behind me. The hard, frigid feeling not doing a damn thing to calm me down. I felt I'd pass out from Billy's stare alone. I recognized he had a small accent, not one that was really visible, but his clear fury, albeit hidden, was still noticeable.

"So, are you the one who's going to come up with that money, Melissa?" He moved a step back, and I sucked in a breath of air. "Because I planned on having a private meeting with both assholes and seeing what they came up with in terms of payment."

He grinned suddenly, all straight, white teeth that reminded me of a creature knowing he had its victim in a death grasp.

"I could never come up with that kind of money." My voice was hardly audible.

"Is that right?" He sounded bored. "What were your intentions by coming here?" He crossed those beefy arms over his wide chest and stared down at me. He inspected me from toe to head, a contemptuous grimace on his face. "Let me guess." He brushed a hand over his face, the sound of his palm scraping over his stubbled jaw excessively loud in the still room. "You're wearing clothes that make me think you're willing to sell your body for a little coin." His voice sounded so... bored.

His gaze was concentrated straight on me. His gray irises seemed so dark it was like a mirror of the pits of hell, I was sure.

"Am I correct in assuming that's why you're here? That's why you wanted to meet me so fucking badly?" He ground his teeth, his gaze traveling up and down my body with a look of utter contempt.

"I–I don't know why I'm here." It wasn't a total lie. I understood my goals coming here, but now, standing in front of Billy, I was questioning every single damn thing.

A scowl covered his features, and I felt my heart drop into the very bottom of my stomach.

"Don't fucking lie to me, little girl."

As long seconds passed by without either of us speaking, I knew there was no other option than the only one he was offering, to be honest because he already knew why I was here.

Like a sadist, he wants me to say the fucking words.

I brushed off the perspiration that was building on my brow. Looking down at my clothes, embarrassment hit me with the feeling I could have pulled this off.

Had I really imagined that I could convince Matte, a blasted crime lord, of anything by wearing revealing clothing?

I lifted my attention and saw him still studying me. I licked my lips and saw how his attention slid down to watch the act.

The corner of his mouth lifted in a sneer, and I took a minute to marvel at how the cloth of his suit jacket stretched across his shoulders. His muscles were evident, and I let the thought of what this large, massively powerful man would look like with no clothing on.

I could just imagine all those strong, defined muscles straining and flexing as he moved. I could see the tattoos peeking out from the costly cloth that covered him, and I thought about how much ink covered his olive-toned body.

I couldn't breathe. I couldn't catch my thoughts as I watched him walk, stalk... saunter closer. And then, he was once again standing in front of me, and I was staring up at his massive, hard body. His glance rested on my eye. The one that had a black and blue bruise covering the side. The one I wasn't able to entirely cover with makeup.

His jaw tensed, the sound of his teeth grinding together deafening in the small confines. When he gazed into my eyes, I saw this blackness in them that had me taking in a sharp breath because a sliver of panic swept over me. This was the look of death. This was me peering into the eyes of the Devil.

I froze.

Out of my peripheral vision, I noticed Billy raise his hand. Instinctively, I cringed away, and I watched the fire in his eyes swell to an inferno.

But he didn't strike me. He cupped the side of my face, his thumb stroking directly under the border of the bruise under my eye.

Gently.

God... so tenderly.

"Who did this to you?" His voice was so low I felt chills of ice race up and down my spine.

I shook my head but wasn't sure what I denied.

Billy moved in close, his mouth now near my ear, so I felt the warm tendrils of his breath caressing the shell. "You'll fucking tell me who did this to you, and you'll tell me now."

I closed my eyes and shuddered for reasons other than uneasiness and terror. I trembled because the feeling of his body pressed so closely to mine made me feel things that tightened areas of me no one had even seen or touched before.

"It's nothing," I finally answered, my voice whisper thin.

His breathing increased slightly, but he didn't answer. He just kept brushing his thumb lightly over my cheek before pulling back and looked into my eyes.

"I know who fucking touched you. I can see the truth in your eyes whether you voice the words." After a second, he backed away, and I sucked in a deep lungful of air.

I wasn't sure what he saw in my expression, but whatever it was, the corner of his mouth raised slightly, and he chuckled.

"Careful, Mellie," he muttered, low and rough. "I can see you thinking about me fucking you, and I may just do that in this piece of shit, dirty warehouse." He grinned. "And I'm the type of bastard who wouldn't care if you cried because I was making you my whore."

I saw something in his eyes, this spark of something I

couldn't decipher. But it somehow softened his comments, made them less ugly and aggressive.

And before I knew it, Billy was standing right in front of me. A little sound left me. Maybe a gulp. Maybe an inhale of breath. Either way, I couldn't contain myself right now.

"Use your words, Sunshine."

The way he used that endearment made something flutter in the most personal portions of my body, a feeling I'd never experienced before. It scared me, made me a little frightened of how much I liked it. But I resented him saying something that could be so nice.

He breathed a gruff chuckle when I didn't answer. He turned and went back to the desk, leaned against it again, and waited.

Just waited.

"My father and brother have done bad things."

"They're pieces of fucking shit, Melissa." He inclined his head to the side. "Why the fuck would you want to help either of those assholes? They don't do stuff for you. They don't provide for you, support you, and they sure as hell don't love you, little girl."

My throat closed up because I knew he was right. "Because they're all I've got in this world"

"I'm going to give you a piece of free fucking advice, Sunshine. You don't need anyone in this godforsaken, filthy planet to save one person." His face got darker... meaner. "Yourself. That's the only person you can count on." He tapped his temple. "Fucking remember that."

The silence stretched out, and the more it remained, the more uncomfortable I felt.

I'd heard enough murmurs and tales about what type of man Billy was.

Thief.

Murderer.

Drug and crime lord.

The list went on and on.

Just do it.

Say it.

"Isn't there something I can do to make things right? Some accord we can come to terms with?"

In the back of my mind, I asked myself why I gave two shits about what happened to Zak and Nash Barry. It was true they'd never done anything to make my life simpler.

Had there been lovely memories of my father and brother? Maybe? If I had them, they were few and few between that they almost looked like fever dreams, things I'd made up to cover the ugliness of how my childhood and life had been.

I couldn't even recall a time before I was five years old. It felt like I'd woken up one day that age, pushed into that awful world where I was looking up at my father and brother as they shared a needle and shot up.

"Something to make things right?" Billy said in a bored tone.

I felt a stray tear fall down my cheek and realized I couldn't do this. No amount of aiding them would change my future. It wouldn't help the outlook of how things would play out.

I forced myself to think of all the times they'd let me down.

When I was seven, my father dislocated my shoulder because he held me too tightly in a drug-induced rage when he thought I was an intruder. Or when I was ten years old and my brother made me buy his drugs from the corner in the middle of the night because he was too much of a coward, scared the dealer he owed money to would see him.

I was upset that I didn't let myself think about all the things they'd done to me over the years, refusing to allow that darkness creep in deep because I still hung on to the belief that family was family and that one-day things would get better.

But after failed treatment attempts, I knew my "family" only cared about one thing, and that was what benefited them.

"Family doesn't even mean anything," I murmured.

I'd been nearly stabbed, battered and burned, and verbally and mentally assaulted by the people who should have loved me and cared for me. They only loved me when it suited them, when they needed to exploit me for something.

I would be better off if they were dead.

"Would you like me to make that possible?" Billy's voice was deep but smooth, like black silk.

I jerked myself out of my thoughts and felt my eyes expand. "W- What?" I'd heard him clear as day, but surely, he didn't mean what I thought he did.

"I can make your brother and father's debt go away with a flick of my fingers." He snapped them as if that proved his point.

I shook my head. I was mortified to allow the concept of them gone for good from my life play through my head.

"Just think," Billy murmured, low and gentle. "They've held you back your entire life. You haven't been able to leave this shithole of a city because there's always something happening, isn't that, right?"

I licked my lips but didn't answer.

He was right. God… he was right. He'd already said he knew stuff about me. Probably all things, if I was honest with myself.

Never enough money. Working tirelessly merely to survive with the bare minimum. My brother or father being sick and the humanitarian part of me feeling a need to care for them.

It was always fucking something.

"This is crazy," I murmured.

I knew what he was saying. He'd kill them for me, bury

their bodies in unmarked graves where no one would ever discover them. "Why would you do that for me?"

This made no sense.

Billy could murder them—probably would—without a second thought.

What did it matter what I wanted?

He was silent for a long minute before giggling humorlessly. "Maybe you have something I want."

Something I want.

This man could have everything and everybody he wanted. All he'd have to do was say the words.

I was no one.

Nothing.

I was impoverished and plain and came from a damaged background.

"I have to go." I turned and reached for the handle of the door, expecting it to be locked. It astonished me when it burst open. The behemoth of a man stood watch on the other side. He focused his eyes on me, but as he glanced over my head, presumably at Billy, he took a step aside and put his attention down to the floor.

"Remember what I said, Melissa."

My heart raced, and I was locked in place, still refusing to glance back at him.

"Sometimes, you have to take matters into your own hands."

His words hung in the air ominously because I knew they signified something much deeper. I just didn't know what.

I didn't look behind me, didn't want to risk Billy telling me I couldn't leave. I all but raced out of that warehouse and into the night, sweat beading my brow because deep in my bones I knew this wasn't finished. I knew Billy wasn't done with me.

Billy

I watched her leave... dashing away from me like a scared rabbit being chased by a fox.

Although I'd known Melissa Barry had been seeking me out, had known from the very first moment she said my name, I'd waited and watched to see how things would play out.

Bringing her to Butcher and Sons, an abandoned slaughterhouse that was now exclusively used for clandestine affairs and unsavory activities, had done what I'd planned it to do, scare the hell out of her.

But despite her being surrounded by this tragedy, she had been so fucking pretty. She was stunning, a brilliant light in contrast to all the dust, gore, rot, and age of this disgusting warehouse.

It was a death hole.

A cemetery.

It was my butcher block.

"Robert," I screamed out, and the man who worked for me opened the door a second later.

Robert, the massive fucker that he was, had to turn to the side to enter the doorway. He was a giant of a bastard, peeking in at seven feet tall and weighing over three-hundred pounds of pure muscle.

I'd found him on the streets of Rome two decades ago, both of us homeless orphans who'd been doing tiny crimes simply to survive.

Back then, he'd been tall and lanky... hungry and bruised up because he often got into fights.

We'd both understood that we were the same, that the world had molded us into these deviants and monsters who would do anything and everything to stay above water.

As we grew older and I established my empire, Robert had been the only choice for my second-in-command.

Irritation seized every cell in my body at the fact that Melissa had come to me, wanting to sell her pussy to me in order to support those pieces of shit men she called family.

I was even more furious about the fact that they had wounded her, that she had a mark on that gorgeous, pristine skin.

I felt murderous.

"I want you to find and bring in Zak and Nash Barry," I told Robert, my voice low, deadly, as I thought of all the ways I'd kill them.

Nice and slow.

Painfully.

Because I knew for a fucking certainty the bruising on her eye wasn't the only time one of those bastards had hurt her.

Robert gave a deep groan in acknowledgment. Although he spoke English proficiently, he rarely uttered it, and when he did, it was as derogatory slurs and swearwords. He didn't wait for me to say anything else, simply turned and left to obey my commands.

It was time to put this stuff to bed, to clear those motherfuckers' slates where I was concerned. I curled my hands tightly into fists, hearing my knuckles crack. I felt my skin stretch over the new scabs that had formed from beating the shit out of a guy two days before.

One of those fuckers had hit her, put a bruise on her. She tried to disguise it and had done a decent job of it, too. But I recognized when someone was trying to disguise abuse and violence. I lived with it before I killed my father for doing the same to me.

And knowing that someone had laid their hands on her fanned a fire inside of me I'd never experienced before. I didn't know if I liked feeling this strongly over a woman. She was a weakness, and I didn't fucking allow myself to have any of them. Especially for someone I had only just met.

What was it about her that made me… desire her so fucking badly?
The innocence that obviously surrounds her?
The fact she was a survivor like I was?

She was gorgeous, but beautiful things always surrounded me, so her exterior look wasn't the beacon that drew me in.

It was just… her.

I curled my hands into fists again and loosened them. I did this frequently until I felt the wrath in me level out so I could think more clearly. There was this demon within me, one who desired blood and murder and revenge.

And I was going to give the fucker a bloodbath.

After an hour, I leaned against the wall in a back room of Butcher and Sons, watching as Zak and Nash were strung up from a metal beam that ran across the ceiling.

It had been easy enough finding where the two scumbags had been. Even if I didn't manage half this fucking town, Zak and Nash constantly visited the same hole-in-the wall and cum-stained floor shops in Desolation.

Robert and another one of my troops had already given the two fuckers a beating. Their blood trickled down the dirty concrete floor. Bruises peppered their faces, arms, and chests.

Zak, her father, looked worse for wear out of the two. When I first came into the room, I believed the guy was dead.

Both had their arms over their heads, a length of rope wrapped around their wrists. Nash was passed out, but Zak was murmuring, imploring in between his gurgling, wet-sounding gasps.

Robert and my other soldier were off to the side, waiting for instructions from me.

I unbuttoned my cuffs and rolled the black cloth of my dress shirt up my forearms.

I'd taken off my suit jacket and tie when they'd first arrived, the apparel thrown over the worktable that held an assortment of torture tools.

I walked up to the rusting table pushed against the far wall and bent down to retrieve the bucket on the ground beside it that held murky water that was probably a mix of bodily fluids.

Once I had it in hand, I stalked over to Nash and quickly chucked that shit in his face to wake his ass up.

Zak tried to lean away from the spray of fermenting water just as Nash sputtered awake.

I cursed at the foul-smelling liquid and took a step back. "Fuck, Robert," I snapped. "Did you piss in this bucket?"

Robert grumbled and tipped his head toward Daly, signaling it was the other man who'd done that.

"Drink more water, fucker," I growled out to Daly.

The crazy man just grinned and pulled a cigarette out of his jacket pocket. "Got some discards from the butcher shop in town. Threw it in there for good measure." Daly stated.

If I had a weak stomach, that might have made me lose my lunch, but I chuckled and remarked, "Well played."

I went back over to the table and ran my fingertips over the different weapons of torture I'd be using on these idiots.

I picked up a pair of brass knuckles, slid them on, and moved back to the two fuckheads.

"You know why I brought you here?" I asked Zak as I glanced at the brass coating my knuckles.

He spoke incoherently.

I glanced up and cocked an eyebrow.

Zak opened his mouth, stuttering a few times before he

found his voice. "I know we owe you money, and I swear we'll get it to you. We've just been trying to win it back!"

I held up my hand, stopping him from running his mouth.

"That's not why I brought you here today." And it wasn't, really.

I didn't notice how Robert's brows pulled down slightly in wonder or how Daly bent his head to the side in curiosity.

I stroked my finger over the metal, the brass rough from the countless times I used it to beat the shit out of men who crossed me.

"I had someone come visit me. Someone that you two pieces of shit know very well."

If the two douchebags could have stared at each other in astonishment, I'm sure they would have done so at that point. But as it was, they could hardly keep their fucking heads up.

"Melissa came by trying to save your worthless asses." I glanced at each of them, remembering her in my office and feeling my fury swell. "Wanted to sell her ass to me to save you fuckers."

"She'll do it. She's a good girl."

I backhanded Nash before he could say anything further that would further piss me off.

"I declined her offer."

Both men groaned and pushed against their bonds.

"I may be the worst of the worst, but I won't let her take the fall for you two fuckers." I ran the brass knuckles along Nash's shirt, wiping off his blood.

"One of you two hit her."

I felt the room still, knowing Robert watched me intently. I wasn't known to give two shits about what anyone said or did. Although I didn't hurt women or children, I also wasn't tolerant when it came to taking out someone who looked at me the wrong way.

"And I have to tell you…" I halted and clenched my teeth,

curled my hands into fists, and snarled out, "seeing that bruise on her face pissed me the fuck off."

I exhaled but kept my fists clenched firmly into balls.

"That's why you two are here. I'm gonna find out which one of you hit her this time, and then I'm gonna fucking murder you before I kill the other one."

Zak opened his mouth, likely to plead for his life, but I swung out and struck the brass with his face. Zak's head cracked back, and he groaned. His cheek split open, and blood poured down his face to seep into his torn and ruined clothing.

"That was the light one. I'm just getting warmed up, assholes. Did Melissa ask you to stop? Beg you to?" I said through tight teeth.

Zak sputtered and shifted his head toward Nash. "H-he was the one," he wheezed out.

My eyesight turned wavy, red engulfing everything in front of me. Before I knew what I was doing, my fists were working in tandem to clock both motherfuckers repeatedly.

"He'll die from blood loss or shock if you don't slow down."

I heard Robert's voice, and his words penetrated the foggy wrath enveloping me. I forced myself to take a step back. I was breathing hard when I came back to my senses.

"You're right," I whispered out, not understanding until that moment how out of breath I was or how much blood covered me. "I better end this now before these fuckers pass out and can't feel how I make the last seconds of their lives even more painful."

I tossed my brass knuckles away and walked over to the old and battered table and grabbed a ten-inch serrated knife. I eyed it, turned to face Zak and Nash, and smirked as I walked over to the fuckers.

Zak was worse for wear out of the two, and Nash was

trying to breathe now as he watched me. I could hear the liquid in every breath he took, possibly blood filling his lungs.

"I need to be quick," I said conversationally. "Sounds like you're about to suffocate on your own fluids."

Because Zak was half aware, I moved up to Nash and grasped his chin, turning his swollen and damaged face up, so I forced him to look at me.

"If you had only owed me money and hadn't put your hands on Melissa, I would have made your death far quicker."

I smelled the perspiration and pee flowing off of him.

I took the blade and ran it over either side of the asshole's face. The skin opened up instantaneously, and Nash shouted in anguish.

"I want to make you and your dad's death slow and painful, but I know you're too close to death as it is." I leaned in and hissed, "And I want you with it enough to know you're dying."

I stabbed Nash in the gut and heard the slimy gurgling of his cry. "Your death won't make her forget how you two ruined her fucking life, but it'll make me feel better and ensure she's safe. Robert," I whispered. "Use the smelling salts on Zak. I want him lucid when this all goes down."

"Billy," Robert muttered, and I looked over at the man I'd been closer to than anyone else and narrowed my eyes. I could see the perplexity on his face.

"Don't fucking say it, Robert," I hissed. I wasn't in the fucking mood for anyone to question my intentions, least of all the only person I'd ever cared two shits about.

Until now.

Robert's nostrils flared as if he wanted to say something, but he clamped his jaw and looked away. I plunged the blade right beneath Zak's ribcage, knowing I barely had seconds before he died.

He gurgled, struggled fruitlessly, and as I leaned in and

stared into Zak's eyes, I smiled slowly as I watched the life leave him.

Zak made one last frantic appeal for life, a sudden gasp of breath, and then he was gone. Nash made an inaudible sound; one a wounded animal would make when it knew it was about to die.

I shifted my attention to him and stated in a low voice, "You're next, motherfucker."

The silence that filled the room was deafening, yet there was also this release that seemed to come from me like I'd never felt before.

I took a step back and stared down at the knife, the blade leaking red, sticky fluid onto the cracked and damaged concrete floor.

When I lifted my head and gazed at Zak's motionless form, I inhaled sharply, smelling the coppery flavor of blood that filled my nose.

A nudge to my side had me looking toward Robert, who held out a bottle of vodka to me. I drank the alcohol until nothing was left, until my throat was numb and my belly full, my head feeling light. I moved the blade up, opening up the prick's stomach like a hot knife going through butter, and pulled it out. Blood dripped from it, landing on my loafers.

"Finish him. Slowly," Robert said as he grinned.

I felt my pulse race as I faced off with the other man.

All I saw was Melissa.

All I saw was the way she wanted to save these fuckers, to sell herself to me and save them.

Fuck them.

I saw red for a long time, until someone pulled me back, and I was staring at the mutilated and sliced up body of Nash, barely hanging from the rafter, a huge puddle of blood below both men and spreading.

"Shit," Daly said as he came closer and eyed the corpses before whistling low. "What the fuck am I supposed to do with the bodies?" Daly pushed at Nash's chest with one finger, causing his body to swing from the ropes.

"Take them to the outskirts of town to the abandoned industrial district. There's twenty acres. I'm sure you can find some place for them," I said in a deep voice.

"You sure no one will come looking for them?" Daly pushed at Nash again, chuckling low when a squirt of blood came out of the gash in the side of his neck.

"Who the fuck cares if anyone comes looking?" I snapped, baring my teeth. "You do as you're fucking told. Understand?"

Daly snapped his head up and looked at me, his throat working as he swallowed. He gave a sharp nod and stepped back, looking at the floor in a subservient gesture.

Motherfucker.

The sound of a lighter swishing open filled my ears, and I watched Robert light the end of a cigarette.

"What?" Robert said from around his cigarette, shrugging.

Melissa

I don't know what woke me up, but I stared at the ceiling, my heart racing, and this sense of dread settled deep within me. I laid there for a moment, listening, trying to calm this sudden fear that had overtaken me.

I heard nothing but my body still refused to calm down, so I pushed myself up on the bed and looked around. My breathing increased, my heart kept racing, and sleep wasn't going to happen.

After scrubbing a hand over my eyes, I stared out my bedroom window. The glass was old and foggy, with a crack in the corner that I'd had to repair with a strip of duct tape.

I figured my father and brother had broken in… again. Although I saw them infrequently anymore unless they had nowhere else to go… or hide from the problems chasing them. If they weren't drunk as skunks or higher than kites and stumbling in, they were hiding from someone they owed money to. Changing the locks or trying to keep my home mine wasn't fixing my problems or keeping them away.

Once again, irritability consumed me for trying to help my father and Nash.

My thoughts became even more annoyed when I realized how foolish I'd been to go see Billy. He could've killed me, or worse. He could've done anything he wanted to me, and I would have been at the mercy of whatever twisted desires he had.

But he let me go.

And for days, I'd been thinking about the why of it all. I sat here for hours on end contemplating all my life's decisions where my father and brother were concerned... where Billy was suddenly concerned.

And it was in the middle of the night that I realized I had to make a change for myself. I couldn't stay in this shitty city any longer. I couldn't risk being brought down even further. My family knew where I was here and would constantly take advantage, so leaving was my only choice.

I wanted to swim to the surface. I wanted to see the light for the first time in my life. So, with that plan in mind, I knew I had to leave Desolation. And I had to do it soon.

I finally said fuck them.

I was going to pack up my shit, take the meager amount of money I'd saved, and just leave.

So here I was, heading into the kitchen in the middle of the night with a smile on my face because I finally felt good for once in my life. I finally felt like I was doing what I was supposed to do.

I didn't know when I'd leave, didn't know how the outcome would play out. I just knew I would leave, and I'd do it as soon as humanly possible.

Drug addicts, pushers and dealers, and crime lords riddled this shitty town. And if you weren't selling yourself on the street corner just to survive, you worked until your fingers bled and your eyes crossed.

If you weren't lucky enough to get out, the other option to leave Desolation was to be buried, more than likely in a shallow grave on the outskirts of town because you fucked with the wrong person.

And that's what was going to happen to my father and Nash. Sooner rather than later, they'd be nothing but memories of a shitty part of my life. And so, I had to get out to save myself because I'd be damned if I allowed anyone to bring me down with them.

I was just pissed that I had waited so long only to come to that realization. But I'd still tried to find happiness amidst an enormous pile of shit.

I stepped into the kitchen and grabbed a glass, turned on the faucet, and filled it up. The water tastes coppery, but it was all I knew and had gotten used to the flavor of blood filling my mouth.

I just stared down at the sink, the basin showing so much age. The faucet only worked half of the time. And the water took a few seconds to turn clear once the water ran.

It only took a second before I felt this tightening on my skin. The hairs on the back of my neck stood on end, and I just knew… knew that I wasn't alone.

I grabbed the dull butcher knife I kept in the top drawer and spun around, my heart already racing as I scanned the small, one room main living area.

At first, I saw nothing, but as my eyes adjusted to my surroundings, I sucked in a quick breath when I saw a large body sitting on the single piece of furniture I owned.

The massive figure was clearly male. He sat in the dark on a chair pressed into the shadowed corner, the darkness shrouding him so I couldn't clearly make out who he was. He was big, though, wearing all black; the night wrapped around him, as if it were familiar with the type of man he was.

It was only after a moment that I knew who sat in the seat before me, watching me, able to kill me before I even uttered a word.

Billy.

For a long time, I couldn't speak, my tongue too thick, my throat too dry and tight. My fingers were curled tightly around the hilt of the knife, painfully so.

I'd never actually hurt someone, never used a weapon for bodily harm ever in my life. And I didn't know if I could start now, didn't know if I could plunge this blade into Billy if he came after me.

But he just sat there watching me, and although I couldn't make out his expression, I could feel his penetrating gaze locked on me.

I heard pum pum. Pum pum. I looked down to see him tapping his fingers on the arm of the chair.

He slowly leaned forward, resting his elbows on his thighs, and a swatch of the muted yellow street light that came through the living room window showed me his face.

My hand shook, my skin slippery from sweat, and before I knew it, the knife fell to the kitchen floor with a clatter.

All I heard was ringing in my ears. I knew without a doubt Billy had come here to kill me. There was no other explanation why he was sitting in my living room in the middle of the night.

How long had he been here?
Why didn't he kill me while I slept?
You fool.
You've heard the rumors.

He likes the torture. He likes inflicting pain.

He probably wants to hear me scream and beg for my life. I wish I was strong and could say I wouldn't do any of that.

But that was a lie.

"Come here, Melissa."

I shook my head, and he tsked and leaned further forward in the chair, bracing his forearms on his knees and staring at me.

"Ah, sweetheart," he all but purred. "Arriverai a capire che negarmi ciò che voglio mi rende solo più duro del dannato acciaio."

My throat was tight and dry, and my head rushed with this intoxicating high that terrified me.

Moisture pooled between my legs despite the fact I didn't understand a word.

"Now, be my good girl and fucking get over here."

My heart raced, and the sound of that promise and violence all mixed was like a shot of heroin in my veins.

This man was dangerous.

He was dominant.

Aggressive.

And here I was, obeying him and moving closer.

When I was only a few feet away, my heart started beating so fast and hard that I wondered if he could hear it, if he could smell the sweat pooling between my breasts and sliding down the length of my spine.

My fight-or-flight instinct was strong, my body screaming that I needed to get far away from the danger.

Yet, my feet stayed cemented in place, my hands curled so tightly my nails dug into my palms painfully.

There was this resolve that settled inside of me. I would not back down. If I was going to die, I would at least do it with my eyes open and my head held high. I might beg. I would probably plead, but I would look him in the eye when he ended me.

"Just do what you're going to do," I whispered those words, not even realizing I said them out loud until they hung in the air between us.

He didn't respond. I didn't even think he breathed as he stared at me.

I moistened my lips and uncurled my fists so I could run my palms up and down my outer thighs.

"And what is it you think I need to get on with, baby?"

I didn't allow myself to think of the endearments. I knew this wasn't a good man.

He was playing with me.

A cat-and-mouse game.

Tossing me in the air just to watch me fall back down to the ground a broken, limp mess so he could continue to do it repeatedly.

"Just kill me." I bit my lip hard enough I felt the skin break, tasted the metallic tang of blood on my tongue. "I know that's what you want to do anyway," I whispered, feeling my whole body shake but was proud of myself for keeping eye contact with him.

I noticed his jaw clench, his expression hard as he looked at my face, spending extra seconds on where my healing bruise was.

"Because that's what you're going to have to do. I won't let you use me."

He didn't respond, just stared at me with an unreadable expression. "It's good you see me as a monster," he finally said.

He leaned back and spread his thighs slightly, his body massive in the chair, dwarfing the size of the small piece of furniture.

"Because that's what I am, Melissa. I'm what nightmares are made of. I revel in it, clutch it close to my heart." His nostrils flared, and I saw a flicker of emotion move across his face. "The world will eat you up and spit you out, so being a mean son of a bitch who kills before being killed is the only way to survive."

He started drumming his fingers on the arm of the chair again. The sound would've been hypnotic if I wasn't already trying to calm my racing heart and dry my sweaty palms.

"My death is the only outcome in this situation." I shook my head, but I didn't know what I was denying, didn't know what I was trying to convey.

The rest of the words were right at the tip of my tongue, ready to spew forth like a slap to his face.

"I won't become someone you sell… another whore in your ledger of money-making schemes."

Billy

For long seconds, she didn't respond, just stared at me as if what I'd told her hadn't clicked, like she didn't understand the words I'd just said.

Finally, she took a step back and then another one. I let her retreat, although there was no place for her to go. I wouldn't let her leave, even if there had been a way she could run.

I waited several days after killing her brother and father and burying them in shallow graves on the outskirts of Desolation to come here, to look her in the face and tell her myself that she would now be mine.

Having their blood on my hands didn't bother me. In fact, I felt stronger because of it.

Torturing them, taking them out, watching their life fade from their eyes, and hearing the last breath they took was therapeutic… cathartic.

I contemplated not telling Melissa I was the one who tortured and killed her family. They'd just never come back, never bother her again.

But I couldn't deny the sick satisfaction in wanting to be the one to tell her I took care of her problem. It probably wasn't the way she ever imagined, although I knew it wouldn't come as a surprise. I was a cold-hearted bastard… and her father and brother were pieces of shit.

She knew the outcome of Desolation, of being one of its citizens and rotting from the inside out.

She eyed the front door but was smart enough not to make a run for it. It wouldn't have mattered, anyway. Even if I didn't have Robert waiting right on the other side, I'd track Melissa, hunt her down like the predator I was.

Pum pum. Pum pum.

I drummed my fingers on the armrests repeatedly, watching her, knowing what her next moves would be and anticipating how I'd counteract them.

"Might as well relax," I said low, deep. "You know you can't run from me, so you might as well be at ease."

She snorted, and I smirked.

"Be at ease? Around a man like you?" She exhaled shakily, her shoulders sagging slightly, but the tenseness and awareness still wrapped around her.

She was smart. Melissa knew not to let her guard down when a monster was right on her doorstep.

And that monster was me. But what she didn't know was I'd never hurt her.

In fact, the strongest part of me wanted to protect her, save her, even if I should have stayed away because I was the biggest danger of all.

Her bruise was healing, but I didn't mention that. She noticed where my focus was, trained on the side of her face by her eye. She looked away and lifted her hand, her fingertips touching the fading mark.

I wanted to kill those bastards all over again, to smell the coppery scent of their blood fill the warehouse, to feel the warmth of it spray across my arms and neck as I gave them their final death blow.

I was a sick motherfucker, but it was the only way I'd been able to survive, the only chance anyone had in a shithole like this.

Snowed in with the Mafia

The little wince that covered her face when she slid her fingers along the mark had me clenching my jaw.

I wanted to dig up those douchebags. My fingers itched to take a knife and go to work, chipping away piece by piece their worthless hides.

I'd feed them to my dogs, but my Tibetan Mastiffs deserved quality, not the scum that Zak and Nash were.

Fuck those bastards.

Whatever she saw on my face had her tensing. I knew she would have retreated even more if the counter wasn't blocking her. I forced myself to relax as much as I could. I didn't need her any more terrified of me than she already was. But even if she feared me, it wouldn't change the outcome of this situation… or her future with me.

And what future was that, exactly?

What the fuck do you want with this girl?

I rubbed a hand over my face and leaned forward once more, watching her, pissed at myself because I couldn't even answer that question.

I didn't know what my intentions were aside from I needed her like fire needed oxygen. I wanted to be inside of her, to feel every inch of her. I wanted Melissa to look up at me with those enormous eyes, so wide and hesitant as I pushed into her tight pussy, as I felt her squeeze around me and heard her cry of shock.

And she would cry out because she was a virgin… because I was too big for her. Because I was too big for her to take comfortably at first.

Something dark and calm settled in me, and I slowly stood, keeping my gaze on her as I moved forward. She reached behind and gripped the edge of the counter, using it to stabilize her because her little body was shaking.

I was a fucking bastard, but the sooner she realized I had no soft edges to me, the stronger she'd be in this situation. And that's what I needed her to be. I couldn't handle her being weak. I didn't want her to break after this was all said and done.

And this was temporary.

She was a means to an end.

An itch to be scratched.

Once my desire for her, this obsessive need to consume her faded, I'd go back to being the soulless, unfeeling fucker that I was.

I was a foot from where she stood. I took a moment to just inhale the scent of adrenaline pouring off of her. Her chest was rising and falling rapidly as her fear spiked.

God, she was so fucking hot as her fear consumed her, yet she stared at me right in the eyes and refused to back down.

My cock thickened, and the urge to reach down and stroke myself like a dirty bastard rode me hard. But there would be plenty of time to show her how depraved I was.

"I killed your worthless brother and father," I said, low, deep, and in an even tone.

For a solid few seconds, she didn't react, but then slowly she changed, her body absorbing what I'd just said. Although, she didn't freak out, not at first.

Her breathing slowed, her pupils contracted, and her shoulders sagged slightly. She looked… relieved.

I couldn't stop myself as I reached out and snagged a piece of her long hair, rubbing it between my thumb and forefinger. The strand was like silk, and I gave it a little tug, then a little harder until her head canted to the side from the force.

"I strung them up like wild animals I'd just taken down in the woods." I kept stroking her hair, and she let me, either too shocked or fearful to react. "I tore them open slowly and made sure they suffered." My focus went to her healing bruise once more. I leaned down and traced the tip of my nose up the column of her throat, scenting her.

God, she smells incredible. She smells like all the good in this world I'll never permanently have.

"And I enjoyed every fucking moment of it, Melissa." Her neck muffled my words. I pulled back and looked down at her, this woman so tiny compared to me.

That appeared to snap her out of whatever calmness she felt because her breathing started up once more, her pupils dilated, and she produced a sound comparable to a wounded animal thinking it was about to be butchered.

"You..." she hesitated, swallowing hard. "They're dead?" Her mouth was slightly open, her jaw slack.

"Deader than dead, baby." I slowly grinned. "I relished every second."

"All over what they owed?" Her voice was soft but monotone, as if she wasn't entirely cognizant of this chat while she sought to comprehend it, work through it.

"Oh, sweetheart." I pulled that strand of hair I still had a hold of to my nose and breathed again before sliding it over my lips. "I would have killed them for looking at me wrong, but that's not why I ended them." I let go of her hair and touched the side of her face.

She surprised the crap out of me by not shrinking back.

"I killed them because of this." I carefully felt the bruise. "I saw this mark, knew one of them had done it, probably not the first time, baby and I had to fucking make them pay."

She blinked rapidly then shook her head. It was evident my actions and motive confused the fuck out of her. I couldn't blame her since I felt the same way.

"You killed them... for me?"

She didn't wait for me to answer as she placed her hands on my chest and pushed me back but not before I felt a zing of electricity crash into me with that brief contact.

"Why?" she whispered and closed her eyes. "Why me?" She kept shaking her head as if to clear it.

I wanted to convince her this wasn't a dream. This was her own personal horror.

I had no fucking notion how to answer that since I didn't know why the hell I was doing any of this either.

"Because I saw you, I wanted you, and I'll do whatever the fuck I want to have you, Melissa."

The air thickened, time stilled, and I knew she was about to flee. What I didn't expect was her kneeing me in the fucking balls. It was only due to my astonishment that she had the upper hand on me.

I groaned and cupped myself as I stumbled back. She darted by me, and I snarled low, irritated that she'd one-upped me, even if it was only this one time.

"Fuck you," she shouted loudly and ran right for the front door.

I would have chuckled at what would await her on the other side if not for the fire and anguish already lodged directly in my crotch from her kick.

I watched as she flung the door wide and was going to sprint full speed. But Robert's enormous figure was standing in her path, and she hadn't paid heed before making her brave escape. She rammed so hard into his back that her petite body jerked backward hard enough she tumbled to the floor straight inside the home.

I heard the snap of her skull hitting the hardwood, followed by her groaning and rolling over. I straightened, a spike of discomfort lancing up the center of my body as if I'd been the one to hit the ground.

I clenched my teeth and tipped my head toward Robert. He stepped inside, closed the door and started to bend down to pick Melissa up.

"Don't fucking touch her," I snapped.

He lifted an eyebrow at me. It was the sole expression on his face as he slowly straightened and stepped back.

She was groaning harder as she struggled to sit up, but I smelled the blood before I saw it on her fingers and spread on the floor.

"Fuck," I cursed and crouched in front of her.

She tried to shove me away, but it was evident the knock to her head had dazed her.

"Get Baxter on the phone and have him come to my place," I whispered to Robert without looking at him, wanting our own physician onsite to inspect her.

"Get the hell away from me." She attempted to sound powerful, this little slip of a girl, but her words blurred together.

This sensation of uncertainty and worry settled in me because she was hurt.

What the fuck is this feeling? Why am I feeling it?

Melissa tried to push me away, but her attempts were pathetic, and I took her effortlessly in my arms, swearing inside. "For such a small thing," I whispered near her ear, "you have quite the kick in you, sweetheart. Clearly, you've kneed lots of men in the balls before."

She mumbled something, and I could tell she was going to pass out, but I worried about a concussion. I hauled ass to the car and shouted at Robert to get the fuck going. For the entire ride to my apartment, I held Melissa like she was mine.

Melissa

At first, I assumed it was a dream.

The blood and violence... death.

I kept seeing my father and Nash hanging from rafters, their bodies disfigured as Billy stood back and laughed.

But I realized that vision wasn't reality. I'd never seen gore and violence at Billy's hands. But I remembered the conversation in the living room.

He stood in front of me as he told me what he did to my father and brother as if it were ordinary chat.

It had slowly sunk in that they were gone, no doubt killed so slowly the last words out of their mouths were the noises of gurgling as blood filled their lungs.

I felt zero sadness.

No regret.

I'd genuinely felt relief... a form of ecstasy that I would never again have to be put in the harsh positions they forced me in. I'd never again have to fend off their fury or defend myself from their drug-induced high and drunken abuse.

Once the shock of that new reality had dissipated, the only thing I focused on was survival.

I remembered everything after that, although it felt like a jumbled combination of bits and pieces from a movie running full speed in my head.

I'd been running on adrenaline after kneeing Billy in the balls. All I'd thought about was getting away. Although, in the back of my thoughts, I knew escape was futile. I knew he'd find me no matter where I was, no matter where I hid.

But I hadn't cared.

I had to get away from him.

I had to at least try.

But then I'd slammed into a big ass concrete wall… or so I'd thought. The beast of a man had been blocking my escape, and my momentum had been so tremendous that I'd thrown backward, landing on the floor and shattering the back of my head.

After then, everything had been a confused muddle in my thoughts, but it was all slowly seeping back like a gentle wave lapping at the coast.

I heard voices. Deep, male ones but I couldn't quite make out what was being said at first. There was a little more chat between the two of them.

I didn't dare open my eyes, didn't want to draw attention to myself any more than I already was.

The voices became clearer the more I laid there and concentrated. "She'll be fine with rest."

I didn't know the voice of the man who spoke, but I didn't have time to sift through my recollections and try to identify it before a warm touch dropped on my forehead.

The fingers were hard yet tender.

"You're sure? Because I'll gut you from navel to throat if you're wrong." Billy's deep voice cut through like a sharpened knife, and despite the harshness of his tone, I felt something ease in me at the obvious concern and lethal promise laced within his words.

The digits caressing my forehead stroked my skin in an almost pleasant manner, and although I couldn't see who touched me, I knew it was Billy. It was an odd experience knowing a man like him didn't feel sympathy or empathy. That a man who could torture and kill two people didn't have empathy yet could touch me as if he worried that I'd break.

Snowed in with the Mafia

I heard them retreat from me then their voices sank low as they mumbled to one another. I couldn't figure out what was being said. The sound of the door opening and closing should have made me feel happy that I was finally alone.

But I wasn't.

I could still feel another presence in the room... I could feel him observing me but he was silent, so still that I envisioned him being a statue. I had the same sensation of his eyes upon me as I did when he sat in my living room, eyeing me from the darkened corner like a devil wanting to possess my soul.

For several lengthy seconds, I regulated my breathing, but I felt tense, and with each passing second, my muscles contracted harder, cruelly. The sense of being dragged down, of sinking into the bed, was nearly too much to handle.

"I know you're awake, Melissa." Billy's voice was deep and dark, silky like the whiskey I was sure he drank frequently.

I didn't open my eyes, didn't speak or change positions. I heard him walk closer, though I could tell the floor was carpeted because of his subdued footsteps. I picked up on the heavy thump of his sneakers on the soft carpet as he approached closer.

When he paused at the foot of the bed, I sensed his presence. It was heavy, like a straitjacket.

Suffocating.

Contradicting.

Yet... comfortable in the same breath.

"Open your eyes."

I did what he said.

Slowly.

I was happy the lights were low, my head hurting now that my eyes were open. I held the blankets hard in my fists, without displaying the pain outward where Billy could see.

He curled his hands over the footboard of the bed, the

black button-down shirt he wore folded up at the sleeves revealing his strong, tattooed forearms.

He displayed no expression on his face, no feeling behind his black, unfathomable eyes. I swallowed, feeling on display as if I were a deer in the center of the woods and could sense a predator.

It was as if I knew I was about to die and couldn't stop it.

He straightened and moved toward a door off to the side. He turned the light on, and I could see it was a restroom. I heard the sink run, and a moment later, he was back out, holding a glass of water.

When he handed it to me, I debated rejecting him, cursing him out, and telling him to let me leave. Maybe even toss it in his face.

But my throat felt like the Sahara Desert, and I plucked the glass from his hands before I knew I was doing it.

I downed it in a clumsy style that should've humiliated me, but it didn't. Water dribbled down my chin and covered my shirt.

He observed me the whole time, and when I finished, he refilled it for me. I was on my third glass when I finally relaxed back on the bed, my belly hurting from being filled, my headache diminishing slightly.

Although I knew he still stared at me, I focused on my surroundings. Dark colors of gray, along with a basic design, ornamented the area.

A fireplace was across from the bed, enormous and scary.

There was only one picture on the wall, one that hung over the mantle and displayed a gloomy figure staring off in the distance surrounded by an eerie forest.

Chills moved over my arms because I could picture the figure was Billy, a demon in the middle of the night sneaking through the dark woodland as if it were hunting for some sacrificial virgin to offer to the very devil himself.

"Baxter left some pain pills and is going to come back in

the morning to check on you. I'm going to have him check in frequently for the next few days."

His voice took me out of my thoughts, and I pondered about his words, that demand settling in.

"Days?" I shook my head which caused my migraine to throb harder. "I'm not staying here for days." I closed my eyes and breathed through the ache.

"I'm going to make sure you're doing okay," he continued over me, as if I hadn't just told him I'm not doing what he said. "Besides, there is a snow storm outside, you are stuck here until that passes."

But on the heels of that... It was unusual seeing this concern coming from Billy. I'd only ever heard whispers of his violence. And I'd experienced it when I offered myself up like a sacrificial lamb, and then learned that out firsthand when he killed my father and brother.

"I don't need any medication." But as soon as those words left my mouth, my head pounded, creeping behind my skull and down the back of my neck, like claws burrowing into my brain.

I tightened my teeth and cringed, hating that Billy witnessed the reaction. I could see this tightening in his eyes, the way his muscles twitched in his jaw as he clenched it shut.

"I'm not a doctor," he remarked in a low, annoyed voice as if I were wasting his time. "But I know you have to get on top of the pain or it's a never- ending cycle." He reached into the nightstand drawer and drew out a little, brown, unlabelled pill bottle.

He popped the cap and poured two pills in his hand before pouring me a fresh glass of water and then holding it out.

When I didn't move to grab them from him, he leaned in close and forced me to press back against the headboard. I could smell him... his fragrance, which was a dark and wild, uncontrolled scent.

That had the pain in my head feeling more evident as something else came over me.

"Christ, Melissa." Billy's voice was icy and steely with no hint of softness threaded within it.

We maintained each other's gazes for a long minute, my heart hammering like a drum.

"Take the fucking medication or I'll force it down your throat."

I wasn't a fool. I knew when to fight and when I needed to survive. And just now, I needed to do the latter.

"I could have hurt you, drugged you, and had my way with you ten times over by now if that was my goal."

I knew he had a point.

A valid one.

Without breaking eye contact, I took the pills he offered. He didn't smile, didn't act arrogantly because he got his way. He merely retained that iron composure as I drank the water and consumed the pills.

And when I was ready to pull the glass away, barely half ingesting the liquid, he placed his finger under the glass, tipped it back, and forced me to finish all of it.

I peered into his dark, deep eyes as I drank every drop. And after I finished, he refilled it in the bathroom before setting it back on my bedside table.

Then he just took a seat across from me, not saying anything, not even breathing.

I didn't know how long he stayed there, but it was long enough that whatever medication I'd taken took my agony away, the edges of the world disappearing.

But it was the vision of him leaning forward and bracing his forearms on his thighs, a slow smirk emerging on his mouth, and the faint sound of him whispering, "Jesus, you're pretty," that was the last thing I saw and heard as I allowed the heavy hands of sleep drag me in.

Melissa

I was sleepy when I woke up, my thoughts blurry, like if I were peering into a TV packed with static. The hum in my head caused me to feel discombobulated and nauseated.

I got my bearings, and the first thing I recognized was that I was alone in the room. My eyes were still closed, but I could sense a silence, one that could only be linked to Billy being gone. His presence was like a bolt of electricity across my cortex erasing all sensible thinking.

I opened my eyes, sitting up slowly, my head swimming slightly before everything became clear.

Calmer.

I gazed around the room, the agony nothing but a small tremor in the back of my skull for now.

I felt wobbly from whatever drug Billy had given me. My body felt tight, like I'd been asleep for quite a while. And because I didn't feel drugged, I had to presume that was the case. I made slow work getting off the bed and padding barefoot over to the bathroom. I was thankful to discover I was still in my clothing from when I'd gone to bed at home.

Although, the notion of Billy undressing me didn't terrify me as much as it should have. I blamed that on the narcotics lingering in my system.

I used the restroom and bent down to sip water directly from the tap. I remained there a moment staring at myself in the mirror, noting the bruise along the side of my face, apparently from when I fell.

I gingerly touched it, but the pills I'd taken must still be doing their job because, despite how horrible it appeared, I felt little more than a soreness.

When I left the restroom, I was still alone, my gaze going right to the bedroom door. My heart was thumping quicker the closer I made my approach to it. I was ready to open it when I looked down at myself. Being barefoot and weaponless wasn't going to aid me in breaking free, but a quick look around the room indicated little that would help with the former or latter.

I started searching through the dresser, then the closet, but it was evident this room wasn't being utilized because I found jack shit in either. No clothes. Nothing I could use as a weapon except from a large lamp on the bedside table that was too cumbersome for me to wield effectively.

I couldn't attempt to go empty-handed. That would be the stupidest fucking thing for me to do, and I wasn't in some movie where I was a ditzy lady who didn't know two-shits about living.

I walked back into the bathroom and inspected the cupboards and drawers. Aside from a couple of brand-new bottles of shampoo and body wash, I came up empty-handed.

Then I rechecked the closet. There were a couple additional blankets on the top shelf, but again, nothing that I could use to beat the hell out of anyone.

I glanced at the light once more, stepped over to it, and took it up. It was substantial, big, yet I unplugged it, removed the shade, and grasped the neck in one hand, shaking it a few times to feel how it felt.

I didn't know how long I could retain hold of it as the bottom was solid metal and an abstract shape, but it was better than nothing. After winding the cable around the base, I made my way to the entrance.

Snowed in with the Mafia

I anticipated it to be locked, but it opened right away… and there wasn't a guard stationed on the other side ready to stop me from trying to leave.

This got my hackles raising and warning bells going off in me.

If Billy didn't have someone watching my door, that meant he wasn't worried about me trying to leave. There isn't any hope for it.

For a time, I just stood there and listened. I peered along each side of the corridor and saw nothing except emptiness, shuttered doors, and a few items of decor.

At any second, I expected Billy and a few of his goons to come down the hall. I was sure there were cameras set all over, ones cleverly placed so that, although disguised, he would know what was happening in every square inch of this prison.

The instinct in me said to run, to move as fast as I could, and get away from the danger. But I recognized the reality of my predicament. I was in Billy's house, and he knew this area like the back of his hand.

I could feel him observing me despite being alone. I had to be intelligent, even if the probability of getting out right now was small to none.

I stared down at my bare feet knowing that even if by some mercy of God, I got outside, I definitely wouldn't get very far.

With one more steady inhalation and exhale, I gazed down the corridor once again.

I took a left, grasping the lamp, my arm already throbbing from the weight, my palms moist from my nervousness.

The only thing I heard was the steady tick-tick-tick of a clock in the distance and the quiet thump of my feet hitting the plush floor runner beneath me.

When I turned the corner, I spotted a set of stairs. I was so near to them that I could race toward it and touch the glossy, silky wood.

But I paused mid-step when I came face-to-face with a man dressed in all black, two weapons strapped at his waist, and the ugliest, coldest expression on his face I'd ever seen.

My heart was thumping so fast and hard. I couldn't hear anything other than the sound of it in my ears.

I clenched my fingers tightly around the lamp and saw him stare down at my weapon.

He grinned humorlessly and then curled his mouth in a snarl of contempt.

I was running on pure adrenaline right now.

We stared at each other for a few seconds, as if time stood still and neither one of us could move.

"Get over here, you little, fucking bitch." His voice was highly accented and as ugly as he was.

On instinct, I took a step back, not realizing I'd done the act until the watch dog came closer, his eyes narrowing, his lips pulling back to expose his teeth.

Although they were straight and white, they seemed sharp.

Like a shark.

Like a predator.

He said something gruff and guttural in a foreign language.

Italian.

"You stupid fucking whore. I don't know what he sees in you."

His voice sent hard shivers down the length of my spine, and I took another step back.

Then one more.

I was about to hurl this fucking light at him and hopefully give myself some time so I could get away.

Billy was dangerous, more so than this man. But if Billy was a calm storm that wrecked, this behemoth was a hurricane. He wanted everyone to know he was coming.

I could see the violence in his eyes. He got off on it. Of that, I was convinced.

Snowed in with the Mafia

He charged forward, and just as I turned, I felt him wrap his enormous hand around my hair, yanking me back hard enough that I shouted.

I reached back with the hand not holding the lamp, automatically trying to lessen the pressure and discomfort.

He kept speaking in Italian, words that I didn't understand but ones I knew were unpleasant.

As I felt tears from the discomfort roll down my cheeks, survival kicked in. With my fingers wrapped around his meaty wrist, I twisted and used all my effort to swing the lamp up.

It clipped him on the side of the throat hard enough I heard him grunt from the hit and lose his hold on me.

He cursed something foul and low under his breath, and I utilized his instant lapse of surprise to slip away from him, the lamp smashing to the floor. I heard the bulb snap, and when I stepped back, shards dug into the bottom of my foot.

But I felt nothing except the drive to survive.

I just got one step before he seized my nape and sank his fingers into my flesh. His hand was like a vise, locking around me so tightly I expected him to crush my spine.

"Stupid, fucking, little girl." He threw me hard against the wall and leaned in close, snarling, "When the boss is done with you, I'm gonna fuck you raw. I don't even care that he'll use you up. I'll gladly accept his sloppy seconds and beat you up while I do it."

I was peering up into his eyes when I saw them widen a trifle as if something shocked him. Then it was the warm dampness that covered my face and neck that I registered.

My ears rang, followed by a large weight landing against my torso before sliding down and dropping at my feet.

I couldn't breathe as I was looking down at a corpse.

My mouth dropped open as I peered at his lifeless face, his dead eyes riveted on me. There was an entrance bullet wound near his temple, and on the other side of the exit wound, the bullet stuck in the wall immediately beside me.

I looked down at myself, seeing the blood covering me. There was so much of the sticky, red liquid flowing down my face, across my chest, and down on my bare feet.

I heard footsteps moving closer, but it was distant, as if I were underwater, slogging through a thickness that was suffocating.

It sought to pull me further down.

"Oh God," I whispered out. "You could have hit me," I caught myself saying and glanced at Billy.

He had an unreadable expression on his face.

"Baby girl, you think I don't know how to kill a man with one shot?"

I blinked.

He stood on the other end of the hall, a revolver in hand and squeezed to his side, the tip pointing to the ground.

I could envision smoke shooting out after he shot… after he blew this asshole's brains out.

"You killed him," I muttered in a monotonous voice, stating the obvious as I glanced down at the dead man.

For a second, he didn't answer, and when I looked back at him, I could see him glaring at the body, his brows slightly furrowed, his mouth clinched.

"He said nasty shit to you." He slowly looked back at me. "That offense alone requires blood as payment." He tucked the gun in the waistband of his trousers, at the small of his back. "But he touched you and caused you pain." He took a step forward. "He all but begged me to slaughter him because of that."

I swallowed roughly.

"I want to go," I mumbled instead of reacting to what he'd just said. It sounded far too… possessive. "I demand you let me leave." I was holding back my tears of rage and fear and… something else, something deeper and pleasant that had me clamping my thighs together.

Snowed in with the Mafia

"You're not going anywhere, Melissa, not until I say you can."

I felt my fury build. The fact he was refusing to let me leave prompted this fire to burn me alive from the inside out.

Annoyance filled me as he drew a joint out of his pocket, lit the end with a lighter he produced, and brought it to his lips. He focused on my eyes as he inhaled. The finish flared a vivid orange.

He retained the smoke in his lungs for a moment, without breaking eye contact, and then moved in closer, putting his hands on the wall on either side of my head, boxing me in.

He exhaled.

That pleasant smelling smoke swirled about me in a haze of dizziness.

But fear kept me stuck in place for lengthy seconds. My breathing became rapid from the adrenaline coursing through me.

He repeated this method until I felt my head becoming lighter, my bones like liquid. He exhaled a cloud in front of me a third time and smirked. "You're mine, sweet girl. Might as well accept and submit."

I didn't know what I was doing until I raised my palm to his cheek. I must have shocked the shit out of him since his head cocked to the side from the power of the smack.

I knew if he'd known what I was going to do, it wouldn't have occurred.

His jaw contracted, and I noticed a muscle tic behind the scuffed-up skin.

I inhaled deeply, my hand hurting, realizing I'd just made a major mistake.

I felt like a frail gazelle and he was the devouring lion as he glared at me with the coldest eyes.

He stroked his thumb along his bottom lip. I noticed I split it when blood coated the pad of his thumb. He gazed at the digit, lifted it so it was between us, and stared into my eyes.

Billy returned his thumb to his lips and wiped it along his mouth again before grasping my chin hard, pushing my mouth open, and shoving it inside.

A frightened sound left me, and I tried to move back, but he snarled low, coming face-to-face with me, nose-to-nose.

"Open your mouth and suck it clean." He was unrestrained… something flavoring his words.

I almost assumed it was heightened arousal, as if me fighting back turned him on. I shook my head refusing him and he bared his teeth like a predator ready for his next meal.

"Open your fucking mouth like a pretty, little girl and suck the blood off." His nostrils flared, and I found my lips closing over the digit, my tongue sliding over the pad.

His whole body clenched before something powerful wracked its way through him. He sighed quietly, his eyelids almost closing fully before he removed his thumb.

"Don't do that again, Melissa, or I'll drag you over my knee, bare your ass, and spank it until you can't sit for a week."

He reached down and held himself through his jeans, the girth substantial in his enormous palm.

And then in a motion too rapid for me to even fathom, Billy had both of my wrists in his hands and pressed to the wall on either side of my head.

He used his entire weight to keep me pressed against the hard surface, caging me in, filtering out everything else, so all I could see, hear, and smell was him.

My head felt light, but my body was heavy, the marijuana smoke going through my veins corrupting every cell so I didn't feel as terrified as I knew I should.

Or maybe that was me trying to excuse why I was growing wet or why my nipples were hard and my heart was beating. Because those two things had nothing to do with fear and everything to do with wanting something I'd never had before.

Sex.

And I knew it would be dark and deceitful and all things terrible with the man in front of me.

Billy leaned forward, and I tilted my head to the side, pressing my eyes tight and pursing my lips. I refused to let him know how he affected me. He only earned my rage and fury.

The delicate brush of the tip of his nose along the length of my neck had shivers pebbling my skin.

"Jesus, you smell good." His voice was hoarse, and I trembled reflexively. "So sweet and soft, so innocent and fragile but a little dirty from the blood of that piece of shit covering you." It was the warm, wet sensation of his tongue tracing the route his nose had just created that caused me to quiver.

"Never been so hard in my fucking life." Those last few words were murmured, as if he wanted to speak them to himself.

All these contradictory feelings had me exhaling in a rush, that gust of air fleeing me before I could control myself.

"I could break you so easily, and that turns me on like no other."

God, the way he spoke in that sexy voice did bad things to me.

He was exhaling and inhaling harder now. "Do you know what you smell like?"

He kissed my pounding pulse point.

He crushed his lower half fully into me, and I gulped roughly at the feeling of the gigantic erection he displayed pressing into my belly.

When I didn't answer, he chuckled quietly.

"You smell like you're going to be mine, Melissa. In whatever way I see fit.

In any way I want."

I tightened my jaw and pushed past my misguided yearning. When I turned my head, he pulled back.

He sported a nasty, arrogant sneer on his face, his eyes roving over my face.

"You sure are pretty with blood all over you." He moved in and placed his cheek to mine, his lips by my ear.

I felt the blood on my face smear from the contact, a slippery sensation that had me closing my eyes.

"I can imagine fucking you covered in the blood of my enemies."

He was sick and twisted, and God help me, but I craved it. *Why is this turning me on? This is wrong!*

He let go of one of my wrists, and I found I still held it above me, bound by an unseen rope. Billy was breathing so hard now. He leaned back and watched while he slid his thumb over my cheek, along my lips, and then inserted the digit within.

I suddenly tasted the coppery tang of the deceased man's blood. My stomach knotted, and I bit down hard enough that Billy growled then smirked.

The evil bastard got off on this.

"You're fucking perfect for me, you little wildcat."

With one last stroke of his thumb over my bottom lip, he clasped my wrist once more.

"Say it," he ordered. "Say you're mine, and maybe I'll be sweet the first time I fuck you, the first time you feel a cock inside of that little virgin pussy."

I peered into his eyes, steadied my breathing, and gave him a smile of my own.

"Fuck. You." I enunciated each word, letting them sink in, allowing them to consume both of us. "I'll never be yours."

That sneer he wore eventually disappeared. His eyes became harder, and I felt his cock throb as if my comments excited him further.

In a move faster than I expected, his mouth was on mine, a ferocious growl from him when my gasp allowed him to glide his tongue between my lips.

I was too astonished to even moan over the fact Billy forced his way inside. I could do nothing except take it.

Snowed in with the Mafia

I should have been fighting, kicking, and trying to claw him. Instead, I felt my body melt at the flavor of him.

His taste erupted on my tongue. His warmth encompassed me. His big body drowned out everything else until all I felt, heard, and smelled was him.

I was just as deranged as he was for liking this, for allowing this to carry on for one second longer.

But still I allowed it.

I accepted it.

He pushed his body even more against mine, and a quiet mewl from me. I wanted to pretend it was in revulsion, but I was embarrassingly moist, heinously aroused. And as he slid his thigh between my legs and elevated slightly so he was rubbing on the softest part of me, I hated how amazing it felt.

Sparks of ecstasy flew through me, but reality came crashing back down when he sucked on my tongue, pulling it into the hot caverns of his mouth and then gently biting it.

I wrenched my eyes open to see him looking at me, pleasure and dominance reflected, and a vision I'd never get out of my head. I tried to turn away from him and break the kiss. I was the one breathing hard now, unable to anchor myself or grasp reality. His flavor became entrenched in my taste senses.

I wanted to spit at him. I wanted to drink a bottle of whiskey just to get his flavor out of my mouth. But I knew that this one kiss was now branded in me irrevocably.

There was nothing but smugness on his face as he took a step back. The haziness cleared, and before I knew what I was doing, I brought my palm up, preparing to hit him again. But before my palm hit, he had my wrist in his hand.

It was a tight hold.

A little painful… which I found exhilarating.

Billy

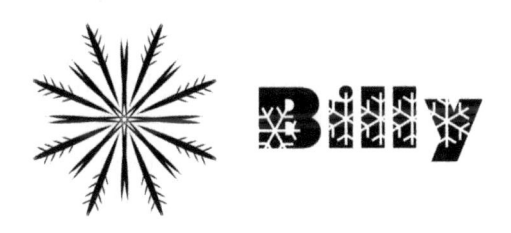

I stood in my office and glanced out the window as I nursed a tumbler of whiskey. I could see Robert down below with two of my other men carrying Declan's body toward the nondescript van.

The entire incident was more of a haze to me than anything else. I'd seen that fucker put his hands on Melissa. I'd heard the terrible fucking things he'd spoken.

I'd only seen red after that.

If anybody was going to touch her, if anyone was going to say dirty things in her ear, it sure as fuck was going to be me.

So, I placed a bullet in that bastard's skull and saw him bleed out all over my fine Italian carpeting.

I wanted nothing more than to toss Melissa over my shoulder, give her tight, little ass a hard smack for wandering the corridors, and then take her back to my room and feast on her pussy as punishment. I wouldn't let her come, either. I would bring her to the edge only to refuse her before jerking off and pouring my seed all over her tummy.

She only got off if she was a good girl.

I made sure she was in her room after I took care of her foot. I didn't have to tell her to shower. She was covered in blood and no doubt wanted that shit off without me saying a word.

But I waited outside her closed bedroom door, hearing the shower kick on moments later.

I kept one of my guys stationed outside when I left. And it would be like that until I could trust her not to be a brat.

I didn't want to keep her prisoner, but I sure as fuck would until she understood that I wasn't letting her go. At least not until I'm done with her.

They dumped Declan's body in the back of the van, and I flung back the rest of my whiskey. Robert glanced up at the window I was in front of and gave me a chin lift of acceptance that he'd make sure everything was finished. And by getting it done, he meant burning the piece of shit in the woods where no one would ever find him.

I refilled my glass and gulped it down in one swallow.

I should have gone to bed.

Instead, I left my office and proceeded to Melissa's room. I waved off the man standing guard. He obeyed without a word.

I stood on the other side of the door and closed my eyes as I envisioned Melissa laying in that large bed. She was a tiny thing, her head barely coming to the center of my chest. But what she lacked in bulk, she made up for in strength and fury.

Yeah... I was a sick motherfucker for opening her door.

It had been a good period of time since she'd witnessed me murder Declan, so I was confident she was asleep by now.

I hoped she was.

I wanted to witness her entirely at peace, at ease. I wanted to see what she looked like with no worries, with her guard down, and not understanding a monster stood over her.

I opened her door, and it swung inward silently. The room was black save from the slash of light entering through a part in the drapes. I could see her little form snuggled in the center of the bed; her tiny, little body covered with the blanket.

The door closed silently, shutting her in with me.

For a minute, I just stood there and listened to her breathing, watching the rise and fall of her chest behind the covers.

I was a sick bastard.

My cock was already erect, all the blood flowing to my groin at the sheer thought of pushing that cover aside and having my way with her.

She'd fight me... absolutely. But I'd never force her, not in the manner she undoubtedly believed. I wasn't a fucking rapist. But her cries, her pleadings for me to stop even though I knew she'd want it, those would turn me on like nothing else.

I found myself at her bedside, not even fucking realizing I'd moved. She was too still to be simulating sleep which made this encounter all the nicer.

I envisioned myself spreading her thighs and licking her out then rising above her and slowly sliding into her. She'd wake up full of my cock, her eyes wide from the penetration, her gorgeous pink mouth gaping as she realized I was inside of her as she slept.

I crouched down on my haunches in front of her. A sliver of moonlight made a beautiful radiance across her small face. I reached out and softly ran my fingers across her cheek, feeling the wetness from her nearly dried tears.

Poor little girl had definitely wept herself to sleep, presumably so upset that she'd become turned on by a predator. And I knew she'd felt that erection when I locked her in. I'd watched her pupils dilate.

I thought about having my wicked, horrible, dirty way with her up against that wall in the corridor. I envisioned sliding my tongue across her cheeks as she cried, pursuing the salty flavor of her tears.

Fuck, I did precisely that.

My face was so near to hers now that I felt the warm touch of her breath on my cheek with every exhalation.

Melissa was totally sleeping, her face relaxed and reflecting how fragile and innocent she was. In this state, she didn't look like the little wildcat I had encountered. She looked like the world could eat her up and spit her out.

I closed my eyes and inhaled deeply; my nose close to her

cheek as I absorbed her aroma. I couldn't help myself as I let the tip of my tongue travel over her silky-smooth flesh. I followed the apple curve of her cheek, traveled along her jawline, and eventually licked at the outline of her lips.

Fuck, she tasted delicious.

I lapped her lips as she slept, the perverse side of me so fucking hard that my cock was pounding behind my slacks. I wanted to slip my tongue inside and memorize the flavor and feel of her.

But I forced myself to pull back.

Although osmophilia had its erotic appeal, when I had her, it would be when she was willing in all ways.

She'd be awake and conscious and look at me right in the eyes the first time I took every single part of her for myself.

I stood, and with one last lingering glance at her, I left the room, motioned for the guard to come back and went right to my bathroom.

I told myself she was a means to an end.

A scratch that needed to be itched.

But in just the short time I kept Melissa locked away like my pretty bird in a cage I wasn't so sure I'd be able to let her go.

I ended the night with jerking off to thoughts of my sweet, little prisoner… and coming harder than I ever fucking had.

Melissa

SEVERAL DAYS HAD PASSED since the hallway encounter where I'd seen Billy shoot a man dead right in front of me. And for those several days, I'd wandered the halls, explored the property with guards trailing closely behind me and hadn't seen Billy at all.

Although, I knew he watched me all the time. He had security cameras set up all over the place, not to mention I knew his goons would report back any time I took a breath.

I sat in the covered gardens and picked at my sandwich. I was utterly alone in this place despite being surrounded by more people than I felt comfortable with.

Asking when I was leaving had fallen on deaf ears.

Could I have tried sneaking off, escaping when I had the first available chance? I could have, but no matter how stubborn and strong I claimed to be, seeing a man's brains blown out in front of me told me to not be a fool.

But I knew, without a doubt, without fail, that Billy wouldn't hurt me. I knew that with a certainty that was so cemented in fact and truth, it was enough to make me bet my life.

Besides, if I tried to leave, how would I get anywhere? Between no vehicle and the blizzard outside, I'm stuck here.

I picked a piece of my crust off and tossed it in front of me. A few birds flew down from the treetops, pecking at the ground, eating up the crumbs. I threw a few more pieces, feeling a smile tilt my lips before they flew off.

I watched them fly higher before landing on the treetops once more.

Of course, I thought about leaving and escaping.

But where would I go?

Back to the only rundown place that never felt like a home?

Who even knew if it was still vacant?

A squatter had probably already claimed it as theirs.

But... that didn't even bother me.

I thought about Billy admitting that he had killed my father and brother. I felt nothing. No remorse or sadness. Certainly, no empathy.

Shouldn't I have felt a twinge of despair over the fact my last remaining family was gone?

I closed my eyes and exhaled, trying to pull at the pieces of those emotions but coming up with a blank slate. I squeezed my eyes shut, forcing myself to remember all the times they had hurt me. Not just with their words but with their hands, too.

I had been nothing but someone they could use. Nothing but someone they could squeeze the life out of because it benefited them.

So, although this was an absolutely beautiful prison, with every day that passed, I felt less like it was. I felt like I was here of my own free will.

And that terrified me more than anything else.

I felt a tingling on the back of my neck and lifted my fingers to touch my nape. I looked around, seeing various employees working on the landscaping. Someone mowed off in the distance. Two others picked weeds to my left. I spotted two staff in the solarium speaking. The man pointed above, and whatever they saw had them both laughing.

Although no one employed by Billy truly spoke with me, I

Snowed in with the Mafia

wasn't met with hesitant glances anymore. I got slight smiles and head tilts in passing.

I rested back on the wrought-iron bench and let my shoulders sag. The sun was warm, a cool breeze from the upcoming change of season brushing over me.

My mind wandered.

A tingling started between my thighs as I thought about the same dream I had been having every night for the past week. I felt myself flush, my body heating at the remembrance of something that had never happened.

I let my eyes slide shut once more and thought about that dream, about how Billy would come into my room and stroke my cheek. He'd push the hair away from my face far more gently than I imagined he could ever be.

He would drag his fingers over my lips, down my throat, and over my collarbones. And then he would kiss me, murmuring deep words. I couldn't understand what he said, but I knew they were possessive.

They were laced with intent and desire and… promise.

And I always woke up hot, wet between my thighs and my nipples hard. There would be this heaviness settled all around me, and it took my breath away.

I continued to rub the back of my neck as the feeling of being watched intensified. I didn't have to make a show of looking around wondering who it was.

I knew.

Was Billy watching me from a window?

Was he standing in front of his video monitors on the other side of the estate stalking me?

Why did that thought make me clench my thighs together?

I made a frustrated sound, tossing the remaining bread on the ground. The birds swooped down right away, and I glanced at them before I turned and made my way back into the house. I passed a few staff members carrying cleaning supplies. I glanced over my shoulder to see two guards trailing closely behind me, their stoic expressions trained on me and not deviating from their task for one moment.

"Assholes," I said under my breath and heard them laugh.

It pissed me off even more.

I hurried to the kitchen, where I planned on getting a glass of water, when I slammed into one of the waitstaff. The tray she carried toppled slightly before she righted it and giggled.

"God. Sorry." I narrowed my eyes at the goons behind me. Both wore smirks. "I'm being followed by watchdogs and not paying attention."

The woman said something to the men in Italian, in which they answered in short, rapid responses. She rolled her eyes and gestured for me to come into the kitchen.

"Here," she said and handed me a small glass bowl filled with what looked like ice cream. "Lemon sorbet. I was headed outside to give some to the gardeners. Looks like you could use a sweet treat."

I took the bowl and the tiny silver spoon, staring at her then at the ice cream in confusion.

"Do I look like I need ice cream?"

She scoffed and looked offended. "Sorbet, Miss Melissa. Homemade by Chef. You won't find anything more refreshing." Someone called out in Italian, and she gave me one nod before heading out of the kitchen. The door swung open, and I saw the goons standing right outside, staring at me.

I rolled my eyes and flipped them off. Right before the door swung shut, I saw them burst out laughing.

The kitchen was blocked off to only this one entryway, so I assumed that's why they hadn't followed me inside since I had no chance of running.

Fuckers.

I sat at the little table that overlooked the gardens from the large picture window. I played with the ice cream sorbet for a second, watching it melt into a silky consistency before bringing a spoonful to my mouth. At that first touch of the cold, citrusy sweetness to my tongue, I held back a moan.

Good God. She wasn't lying.

I watched a few birds land on the bird feeders positioned on the other side of the window. I finished half the sorbet before I felt someone enter. I assumed it was the young woman again.

"You were right. This is the best thing I've ever tasted."

"You haven't had my cock in your mouth yet."

My eyes widened. I spun around in the chair to see Billy standing inside the entryway. "The hell?" I choked out those two words.

He was in front of me before I could even blink, reached out and took the spoon, and scooped a dollop of sorbet out of the bowl.

While holding my gaze with his, he brought the spoon to his mouth and licked it clean. "Mmm. It's good. Sweet." He took another spoonful before setting the utensil down on the table with a resounding clank. "Bet your pussy is sweeter, though."

I choked on my saliva and was about to curse him out, maybe push him away, but none of that happened. I sat there and stared into his eyes wondering what the fuck was going on.

"I'm not staying here." That's what I said. After hearing Billy talk about eating me out, of course, my brain spewed forth those four words like they made any sense in this situation.

"You'll have dinner with me and we'll decide what's going to happen next."

And just like that, the spell and haze broke.

I knew he wasn't expecting me to answer. I didn't know what to say anyway. So, I stayed silent, held his gaze, and refused to break the stare down, and finally, he turned and left.

I sat there scared as hell, wondering what he meant by those words.

Billy

I WAS tired of fucking walking around Melissa like she wasn't going to be mine in the end.

I was tired of waiting.

I wanted her with this fierceness that rivaled anything I'd ever felt before. Wanting her was such a tame fucking way to describe the level of obsession I felt for her. And the longer she stayed under my roof and denied me, the more I watched her, knew her every move, and jerked off to thoughts of her, the more that need grew in me.

I'd barely touched her. Those late-night sessions where I snuck in her bedroom and touched her skin and gently tasted her lips were just teases. She set a fire in my blood the likes of which I'd never felt before.

What I didn't realize was how fun it would be to have her under my thumb. To make her do what I wanted.

To use her.

It made little sense in my world, not in the way I held myself in control. I was used to people cowing to my will. I expected it. That's how I got my power, how people did what I said without thinking.

But everything was different where Melissa was concerned. Everything was different in me because of her, and it pissed me off.

Her very presence threatened to unravel my restraint and

all the fucking shit I'd done in my life to build the world around me. I had to wonder just how far I could push her and how much she'd give in before breaking.

I was a fucking bastard. I revelled in it and wasn't sorry one fucking bit.

I'm sure she knew that, but I doubted she knew the extent I went to for what I wanted.

That's what this little dinner was about. I wanted to see how far my girl would go when I offered her freedom. Would she accept and submit or slap me in the face?

I heard her enter the dining room, breaking my thoughts so I was now fully consumed by the very sight of her.

Although I knew she had an array of designer clothes in the closet, she opted to wear a plain sweater and a pair of dark leggings. The girl didn't even wear shoes as she tipped her chin up and padded to her place setting.

She sat down but didn't look at me.

"I think it's fucking cute you think dressing down and being barefoot for dinner doesn't have my cock hard."

I grabbed her wrist and brought her hand over to my lap. I placed it right over my hard as granite cock.

She snapped her head in my direction, her mouth parting and her eyes wide. She didn't pull away at first, and I forced her to curl her fingers around my girth.

"You could wear a burlap sack and I'd be rock hard."

She ripped her hand away then but not before I saw how her fingers shook as she reached for her water glass.

I didn't push her in that moment, although I really fucking wanted to. I wanted to see how far she'd bend to my will, how she'd submit so beautifully to me.

The food was served, and once we were alone, I started eating, but my mind was churning with all the things I could do to make my little flower feel a little off-kilter.

I took my time eating and waited until she finished. I

could see how nervous she still was, as if she were waiting for me to break the news that I was about to kill her and that's what this whole dinner charade was about.

Far from it, my pretty girl.

"What did you want to talk about?" she asked with a hesitant lithe to her voice. She refused to look at me as she picked up her wineglass and took a small sip. Then another. And another until she finished it.

I reached for the bottle and topped her off without saying a word. I finished my whiskey, but instead of going for another, I drank water. I didn't want to consume so much that I couldn't fully appreciate tonight.

"I want you," I finally said.

I had to give Melissa credit. She showed zero reaction to my words.

"You can't have me," was her response a moment later.

I smirked, even if she wasn't looking at me.

Funny girl thought I didn't get what I wanted.

I always did.

I always will.

"Want to make a wager that you're wrong and I'm right?"

She snapped her head up to look at me then, her brows furrowed, her pretty little face showing deep thought. Then, she touched her lips and looked away.

Awe, sweet, little Sunshine was thinking about those dreams of hers, no doubt.

I leaned forward and braced my forearms on the table, staring at her hard enough that I knew she had to feel it.

"What do you want?"

She took a second before staring at me in the eyes. "Nothing from you." "Everyone has a price."

She scoffed and crossed her arms over her chest. A clear defensive posture. "I'm not a whore and can't be bought."

I chuckled. "Everyone can be bought."

She shook her head but said nothing.

"What about your freedom and enough money that you never have to worry about it again?"

Her entire body tensed. "I won't be a whore for my freedom." She looked at me again. "Just let me go. You can have anyone you want. I'm no one special."

I had her throat in my hand a second later.

Her eyes widened; her jaw slackened.

I wasn't hurting her, I wasn't using enough pressure to cut off her air supply, but I held her tight enough that she would know who was in control.

"I thought I told you not to fucking talk about yourself that way." I felt her swallow beneath my palm and stroked her pulse point with my thumb.

"I could let you go, but I'm a bastard. I'm selfish, and I want something in return."

She lifted her hand and placed it over my wrist, adding a bit of pressure to remove my hand.

I shook my head, and she let her fingers fall away. "Something in return?"

"Mmm." I thought about all the things I wanted in return. "You know what I want." I let my gaze travel up and down her body. "I want you to be my whore."

Her jaw dropped open before she hastily closed it shut. "You're literally insane."

I shrugged, not contesting that.

"I could escape."

I grinned slowly. "You could but you won't."

She narrowed her eyes. "So confident."

"In all things, yes. But especially this." I inhaled deeply. "I know your perfect, little cunt is wet for me."

"You're a monster. A filthy, vile motherfucker."

"I've done enough horrible shit that there's a place in hell for me, but fucking my mother wasn't one of them."

She seemed stunned by my statements, and when I smirked, she let out an incredulous laugh.

"Crazy. That's what you are."

She massaged her eyes and glanced forward. "I'll escape. I'll get out of here and go away from this stupid metropolis and never look back."

I appreciated her courage and strength.

It turned me on.

Everything about her turned me on.

"You could deny me, and I could keep you here forever, if I wanted to. I could not offer any deal and lock you away like my personal little beam of sunshine." I leaned in so our mouths were so close I felt her breath against my lips. "I'd come visit you every day, needing that dose of warmth and light only you can provide."

Her eyes widened in amazement of my remarks.

They stunned me, too.

They were too kind, too lovely for the likes of me.

"But I don't want to snuff out your brightness, Melissa." With one more sweep to her pulse point, I relinquished my grip on her throat and leaned back. "So, I'm giving you the deal. A choice."

"And if I say no, you'll keep me locked away?" She rubbed her throat, but her hand shook, her pupils dilated, and her breathing sped up.

I bet her cunt was wet for me.

I thought about her question for a moment. "I don't know what I'd do with you." It was the truth.

I stated I wouldn't want to snuff out her light, and keeping her my prisoner would accomplish just that. I didn't want her to dislike me…and I didn't understand why.

But I knew thinking about her being gone made something awful rise in me. "This is a good deal for you."

She snorted and I smiled. Genuinely.

"Coercion isn't a fucking choice."

"Touché, Mellie."

"And you killed my brother and father. How can someone get over that and sleep with that person?"

"You say thank you for taking out those worthless fucking pieces of shit who hurt you. Take what I'm offering and then leave Desolation at the conclusion of our arrangement, if that's what you choose."

The fact of the matter was, I was telling her she could leave after all was said and done. But the thought of her gone infuriated me to the point I wanted to fucking shatter something.

As she mulled things over, I decided one more glass of whiskey wouldn't hurt. I sipped on it carefully, letting the warmth consume my stomach. After dinner, the waitstaff arrived to clear our place settings and, a moment later, returned back with dessert.

Chocolate cake with whipped cream and fresh strawberries sat in front of both of us.

Once we were alone again, she sighed and leaned back. I could see the resignation and acceptance on her face.

"You were eager to give me your body when it would help those two fuckers. I'm disappointed you're not doing the same for yourself."

I was an asshole for pulling that card. But I was anxious for her.

Melissa looked at me and asked, "How much?"

I wanted to fucking grin that she gave in, but I kept my expression blank. "How much do you want?"

She scoffed again. "So generous with your money. It's like you have a bottomless pit filled with cash."

"I do," I answered without hesitation.

"How do I know you'll keep your end of the deal?"

I didn't answer as I got my phone out and dialed my attorney. He picked up immediately. "Open an account for Melissa Barry. I want it available solely to her." I rattled off the amount to be deposited into the account immediately. "Put the same amount into the account in two weeks." I ended the call and laid the phone aside.

"That's... that's an insane amount of money."

"More than you could spend in five lifetimes. But it'll be yours after two weeks."

I went back to sipping on my whiskey.

"And w-what do you want from me? Like exactly?" She licked her lips and started shifting on the chair.

"Whatever the fuck I want to do with you, Melissa. You'll be mine in any way I see fit."

"I don't want to be hurt," she muttered.

I squinted my eyes and shook my head. "Have I hurt you?" It only took her a second but then she shook her head slowly. "I could have ten times over by now. But I've cared for you, purchased you everything you needed, and haven't made you do anything you didn't want to."

"Keeping me here contradicts that."

Sassy, fucking lovely girl. God I fucking want her!

I didn't answer and didn't tell her I'd been sneaking into her room at night to touch and lick her and watch her magnificent ass sleep.

"I want to fuck you. Plain and simple. I want that cherry between your legs. I want your virgin blood to coat my cock when I take it for the first time."

I finished my drink and leaned forward again. "And I'll do all of that and more every day I have you here until I'm so ingrained in your head and body, you'll never get rid of me."

I could see how my remarks touched her. They ticked Melissa off, but below all of that, I saw something else.

Desire.

Curiosity.

Compliance.

I knew she was moist. I knew she'd agree. But she was too

proud to cave that easily. Her resisting me at every turn, thrilled me like nothing else in this fucking world.

"Use your words."

Her mouth clenched, but she gave in. "When would this all start?"

"You're stuck here because of the snow outside anyway, so as soon as the words that you agree come out of your mouth."

She licked her lips and murmured, "Okay. I agree."

Billy

I ALLOWED the weight of Melissa's words to settle into the very fabric of my being. A tension hung in the air, an unspoken desire sparking between us. My arousal burgeoned within me. Silently, I leaned back in my chair, absorbing the emotions playing across Melissa's face as she grappled with the unexpected turn of events.

Her confusion deepened as she fixated on the untouched cake, her small yet exquisite frame betraying the turmoil within. Just as she poised her fork to dive into the sweetness before her, I intervened, halting her with a single utterance.

"Stand up."

A flicker of disbelief painted her features, her petite form responding instinctively to my command. Beneath the surface, defiance lurked, an ember waiting to ignite. Melissa possessed strength, but in that moment, I reveled in the knowledge that my dominance eclipsed her will.

"You agreed to this," I reiterated, my voice a low murmur that echoed with a subtle authority. "And it starts now. Part of that agreement is you doing what I say when I say it."

Behind the restraint of my slacks, my cock asserted itself, a robust, steel rod yearning for more than mere acknowledgment. My fork hovered, waiting for her to obey.

As she rose tentatively, the scrape of the chair against the floor underscored the gravity of our unspoken pact.

"Stand in front of me," I firmly directed, my movements

signaling her to the space I desired her to occupy. I observed a tremor coursing through her, wondering if it danced on the delicate line between fear and anticipation. Perhaps, I mused, it was a sublime fusion of both emotions.

Yet, she hesitated, halting shyly before me. Unwilling to let her resistance take root, I seized her hips and drew her closer, my fingers exploring the contours of her delicate form. Nervous breaths escaped her, accentuating the allure that drew me in. Melissa's diminutive stature demanded a measured approach; I resolved to be gentle, careful not to shatter the delicate beauty I held in my grasp, but just a firm enough hand to get her to comply.

After savoring the pulsating energy between us, I spoke, my words a command that hung in the air like a promise. "Take off your clothes and sit on the table. Legs spread." Clearing space by moving the cake aside, I leaned back, granting her the freedom to comply.

Her high-pitched inquiry sounded between us, and my attention momentarily drifted to the intricate dance of her throat muscles. The imagery of her swallowing, her mouth accommodating my desire, fuelled the fire within me. I envisioned the struggle, the deep penetration that would leave her gasping, her eyes watering as I thrust my cock deep in her throat.

"Mmm," escaped my lips involuntarily, a subtle affirmation of the vivid scenarios unfolding in my mind.

"Here?" she whispered, her eyes scanning the surroundings.

Unfazed by her question, I maintained my gaze, wordlessly urging her to embrace the vulnerability of her nakedness. "No one will come in," I assured, my voice a velvet promise. "But even if they did, you could appreciate a little exhibitionism, darling girl."

Her silence echoed through the room, met by the ghost of a grin on my lips. I unzipped my jeans, revealing the pulsating evidence of my desire. Melissa's eyes widened, her tongue tracing the contours of her lips in a subconscious acknowledgment of the burgeoning tension.

"Now, let me see what I own, Mellie."

Her eyes closed briefly, a silent battle raging within. Eventually, she relented. Shyness and nervousness enveloped her as she shed her garments, each piece a testament to her vulnerability.

First, the shirt surrendered, then the pants, and for a suspended moment, she stilled.

Her presence stole my breath away, and silently, I urged her to persevere. "Go on, dear. Be daring for me."

Melissa lifted her gaze, meeting mine with a determination that resonated. Behind her back, she unclasped her bra, letting it fall gracefully to the floor. My cock throbbed in tandem with my racing heart as I feasted my eyes upon her perfection, a goddess in human form.

The climax of anticipation reached its zenith when she hooked her fingers under the edge of her underwear, peeling them away. Leaning forward in rapt attention, I seized the moment when she hesitated and took control.

"What's this, you pretty little liar?" I murmured, my finger tracing the fabric that bore witness to her intimate secrets. Her panting breaths, her stiffened nipples, all heightened the intoxicating allure of the moment. "I'm an ass and nipple man, Melissa," I declared, my self-indulgent strokes mirroring the rhythm of her arousal. "And yours is the most perfect set I've ever seen."

A muted response emanated from her. Conversation wasn't the goal; rather, I sought to test the boundaries of her resistance, to ascertain the depth of control I wielded.

With a husky command, I laid bare my desire for her and her alone. "Now, take off your underwear, sit on the table, spread your legs, and let me see your pussy while I enjoy my dessert."

The air between us thickened, pregnant with the promise of desires yet unfulfilled. Melissa, now exposed and bare, stood at the precipice of surrender. Her eyes, a mirror reflecting the tempest within, met mine, and for a fleeting moment, time seemed to hesitate, caught in the gravity of our shared desires.

"Let me see your pussy while I enjoy my dessert," I murmured, my voice a low, seductive cadence that resonated in the charged atmosphere. The words lingered, a command that echoed through the space between us, stirring the dormant flames of longing.

As she tentatively seated herself on the table, legs obediently parting, a ripple of excitement surged through me. Before me was a masterpiece of vulnerability and submission. I reached for the untouched dessert, the fork poised at the edge of the cake, its sweetness now a metaphor for the impending exploration of forbidden pleasures.

The candlelight danced in her eyes, casting shadows on the canvas of her exposed skin. With each flicker, a new layer of intimacy unfolded. I could sense the rhythm of her breath, a melodic accompaniment to the unspoken poetry that unfolded between us.

"Mellie," I whispered, the endearment of a caress that hung in the air. "Your beauty is a revelation, a symphony that resonates in the silent spaces of our desires." I traced the fork along the contours of the cake, each movement deliberate, an extension of the unspoken connection that bound us.

She, vulnerable yet resilient, met my gaze with a courage that stirred the depths of my being. As my eyes lingered on the delicate canvas of her exposed femininity, I marveled at the intricate brushstrokes that comprised the masterpiece before me.

I dipped the fork into the cake, savoring its sweetness as if it were an offering from the gods of passion. The taste

Snowed in with the Mafia

lingered on my tongue, a prelude to the forbidden feast that awaited.

"Melissa," I breathed, the syllables a whispered prayer. "You are the muse, the embodiment of desire that has danced in the shadows of my dreams." The words, heavy with sincerity, hung in the air, intertwining with the charged currents that pulsed between us.

With deliberate intent, I let the cake crumble in my mouth, each morsel a communion of senses. The sweetness mingled with the heady scent of arousal, creating a symphony that resonated with the unspoken promises of the night.

"Open yourself to me, Mellie," I urged, my words a gentle command. "Come closer, my love," I beckoned, the endearment a prelude to the crescendo that awaited.

She moved toward me, the space between us diminished, and as our bodies converged, the room became a sanctuary of whispered promises and the echo of shared breaths.

I reached out, fingers tracing the contours of her skin with a tenderness that belied the underlying urgency.

Her breath caught in the delicate space between us, a silent acknowledgment of the uncharted territory we were about to traverse. The connection, a thread of electricity, hummed in the air, uniting us in a dance that echoed the rhythm of our hearts.

"Mellie," I breathed, my voice a murmur that lingered in the hallowed silence. "Your vulnerability is a work of art that unfolds in the sacred spaces between us."

I cupped her face in my hands, fingertips tracing the contours of her lips as if decoding the secrets hidden within.

"Feel my touch, Mellie, feel it excite you," I murmured, my breath a soft breeze that caressed her skin.

As if in response, she closed her eyes, surrendering to the symphony of sensations that enveloped her.

"Lay back again," I demanded. I guided her to lie back on

the table, the cool surface a stark contrast to the warmth of our burgeoning connection.

"Open yourself to the music of the night, love," I whispered, my words an invocation that resonated with the beating hearts of two souls entwined.

What is it about this damn woman?

Who the fuck is giving me this poetry shit to say?

Her eyelids fluttered open, revealing pools of uncertainty and anticipation.

Longing.

I began to explore the landscape of her body. Each touch, a note in the serenade of passion; each kiss, a stanza in the poetry of our forbidden dalliance.

Melissa, my muse, surrendered to the embrace of vulnerability, her essence woven into the fabric of our clandestine affair. In the silence, the world outside ceased to exist, and we revolved around the pull of desire.

Melissa's body responded to my touch more than I thought she would. I traced the contours of her skin feeling goosebumps break out across her. Her mouth parted, begging me to kiss her.

As my lips caught hers, our kiss became a sonnet—a composition of desire and surrender. The taste of her, a forbidden fruit, lingered on my tongue, a sacrament shared in the shadows of secrecy.

"Mellie," I whispered against her lips, my voice a velvet murmur that echoed through the sacred space we had created. "I want you."

Her response was a sigh, a melodic note in the composition of our shared intimacy.

"Feel the pulse of my desire for you, Mellie," I urged, the words a whispered plea that resonated with the essence of our connection. I captured her hand, guiding it down to my cock, letting her feel how hard I was for her. Her response, a subtle arch of her back, spoke volumes—a silent affirmation that she, too, was immersed in the ebb and flow of our shared passion.

I guided Melissa into a sitting position, her legs hanging off the table, spread wide. I pressed my cock against her as I reached for her discarded cake. I pick a piece off the slice, offering it to her from my fingers. I watched as she took it delicately, her tongue licking my fingers clean, making my cock pulse.

Melissa

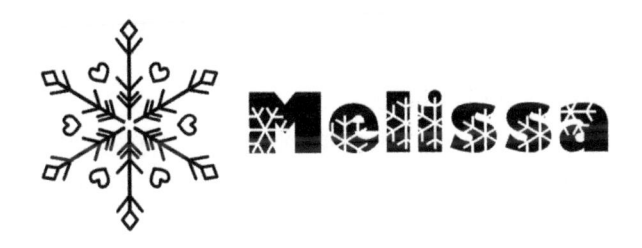

I should have taken the fork and slammed it in his dick, which he was obscenely rubbing in front of me. What he wanted me to do, what he wanted from me, was disgusting, sick, and coming from a dangerous man
who was a narcissist.

Then why did it turn me on?

I stood there for what felt like an eternity but Billy did nothing except masturbate as he sat there watching me.

I hated how that made me feel.

He'd humiliated me by revealing the evidence of my desire.

Getting on the table was one of the hardest yet easiest things I'd ever done. A blatant contradiction in every manner.

Once I sat on the table, I kept my legs closed, dangling them off the edge, feeling my arousal no doubt making a wet area just beneath me. I wanted to cover myself. I'd never gone entirely nude in front of anyone.

"Open your legs and place your heels on each corner. I want to see those gorgeous petals unfolding for me so I can see just how pink you are."

His voice was low.

His tone was even.

Like he knew exactly what he wanted.

Me.

I moistened my lips then pursed them as I knew what I had to do. I agreed to be his for a ludicrous amount of money.

For my ultimate liberation.

I really am his whore.

But the prospect of being able to go anyplace in the world and leaving this shithole city behind was too much of a temptation to pass up.

Even if I had to give my body and soul to the Devil to make that happen.

I placed my palms on the table and elevated my legs, doing what he said by resting my heels on either corner.

But I couldn't look at Billy. So, I glanced up the vaulted ceiling, counting the crystals in the chandelier while I felt a mixture of frigid air and warmth from the fireplace just feet from where we were.

But as the seconds went by and he didn't talk, didn't even touch me, I mustered my confidence and stared at him.

Billy leaned back in his chair, his gaze centered between my legs, his elbow braced on the armrest of his chair as he stroked his thumb along his bottom lip.

I licked my lips but couldn't find the words to either tell him I couldn't do this, to fuck off, or to touch me because I felt like I was dying on the inside if he didn't.

After what felt like an eternity of stillness, Billy pushed his chair closer, slid his dish of cake between us, and started eating.

"W-what are you doing?" My voice was threadbare.

He was silent for long seconds, savoring his cake, as if I weren't sitting directly in front of him with my pussy on full view.

"I'm enjoying my dessert while your pretty pink cunt is right in front of my face, Melissa. I thought that was clear."

The gentle clink of his fork hitting the plate every time he received a forkful of cake seemed overly loud, making my ears ring.

I adjusted my legs, but he snapped his attention up to me, a scowl on his face. "Don't move."

I was so surprised by the loud, whiplash-like tone of his voice that I froze. He went back to his dessert, and I breathed a tense breath.

And God help me, but as the minutes passed by and he kept silent, sporadically eating and glancing between my legs, I felt my yearning swell. I felt my juices flowing down the crease of my ass. I felt the wet mess I was making on the tablecloth. I found it startling at how much I was getting off by this. It was something I'd never acknowledge, maybe not even to myself out loud.

I felt a teardrop slip down my ass and gripped my inner muscles by instinct. This was terrible torment, but God... it was hotter than hell.

Could Billy smell how wet my pussy was?
Could he see how completely hot I was for him?

Once he was finished eating, he moved his dish to the side and reclined back in his chair. His cock was so erect and still free of his pants. The thickness obscenely pointed up; clear fluid spread along the tip.

"You made a big fucking mess on the linen, sweet girl."

He took his handkerchief and dabbed the corner of his mouth.

I was riveted at the sight of his tattoos on the back of his hands, his wrists, and forearms. He had the sleeves of his dark button-down rolled up his arms. With my glance, I traced the scary ink that disappeared beneath the material.

He peered into my face for a suspended minute before snatching his mobile, pointing it at my pussy, and clicking a picture.

I made a surprised sound but was too astonished to move or talk.

"Material for the spank bank?" I could hear the outrage in my voice, and he smirked but didn't respond.

Instead, Billy stroked the pad of his finger over his dessert dish, gathering chocolate icing, and bringing it to my mouth. "Suck on it like you'll be doing to my cock soon enough."

My eyes felt large as I stared at him. My mouth parted in amazement at his words. He took it as my compliance before he slipped the digit past my lips and stroked it over my tongue. The flavor erupted on my taste buds, and I involuntarily did what he said and sucked on his finger.

"Brava bambina." He had mumbled those two words, all the while staring at my mouth.

My nipples hurt, the small beads tighter and harder than hell. I was seconds away from imploring him to touch me, to relieve this fire I felt deep within me.

And I thought he may. I watched as he clenched his hands into tight fists, his knuckles white as he kept staring at me. His jaw was frozen, a muscle clenching under the heavy scruff covering it.

But he rose from the chair and just stood there for a time looking down at me. I allowed myself to take in his big, imposing physique. I ran my glance over how he filled out that dark shirt to perfection. His shoulders were so big and his chest broad enough that it blocked out anything behind him. And when my eyes rested on the huge erection he had, I felt more wetness drip from me.

He may not have touched me, but I influenced him in the most primitive way a woman could a guy.

"Go to bed, Melissa."

Confusion suddenly flooded me. "You're... you're not going to..."

I couldn't actually voice the words.

You're not going to fuck me?

You're going to leave me in this state, so turned on and desperate that I wanted a murderer to fuck me right here on the dining room table?

Maybe he noticed my thoughts washing across my face because he took a step nearer me.

"So ready for me," he murmured deep and low and so damn seductive that I couldn't hold in my moan.

He didn't wait for me to say anything. I didn't even think he was seeking some type of response or reaction.

And then Billy leaned in, and slid his tongue over my lips in a possessive, proprietary fashion. He slipped himself back in his pants and turned to go.

I sat there absolutely naked, watching his disappearing figure, and questioning myself what in the world I got myself into.

Melissa

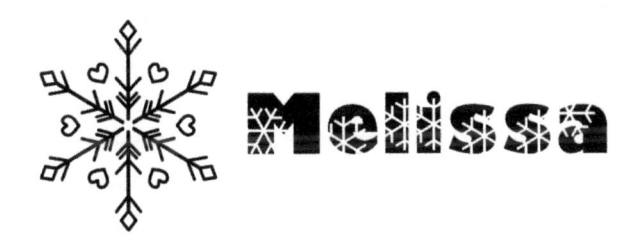

I HAD THAT DREAM AGAIN. The one where I felt him touch me, felt Billy sliding his lips and tongue across my face and neck. It felt so amazing.

He feels so amazing.

I stretched, my eyes flickering open as I gazed into the black room. I could see it was still the middle of the night by the lack of light streaming through the split in the drapes. The bedside clock showed it was just past midnight.

I sat up and pulled the stray hairs that had fallen out of my ponytail from my face. My heart was thumping a little quicker, and I was sticky between my thighs.

The dream had been so vivid although, in my mind's eye, I couldn't see anything beyond his massive, hulking body hovering over mine.

I couldn't focus on anything but the sensation of his fingers and tongue on me and how I wanted to scream, screw it all and let Billy have his way with me.

I peered around the room, feeling that tightening on the back of my neck as if I weren't alone. But I saw nothing aside from darkish nooks and a lot of emptiness.

After using the restroom, I made my way back to the bed and sat on the edge, but I still felt that tingle on my nape. My breathing quickened up as the sensation intensified.

I wasn't alone. I understood that down to my marrow.

My entire body was stiff, and my skin sent tingles up and down my body.

"You look beautiful in any light," the deep, dark voice murmured from behind me.

I was pleased with myself for not moving and for not displaying any apparent sign that he shocked me, that I was a little terrified, or that I was so excited my inner thighs were sticky because of it.

"Look at me," he urged.

I closed my eyes and didn't move for lengthy seconds. Finally, because it was as if his words were this tether and he dragged me to do his bidding, I shifted on the bed and faced forward. At first, I saw nothing, but the longer I stayed there, the more my vision adjusted to the murky interior.

Then I noticed him standing in the corner, his gigantic bulk fitting in with the shadows as if he were designed for the night.

"You like creeping into girls' bedrooms and watching them sleep?" My voice was soft, my words holding zero accusation or heat.

How would he feel if he knew I was getting more turned on by the fact he stood there watching me?

"I like watching you, Melissa." He walked out from the corner but was still cloaked in blackness. "I like watching you every night."

I envisioned him smirking just then, as if he knew something I didn't.

My lips tingle, and I caressed them, sliding the pad over my bottom lip as everything slowly sank in.

He came closer until he stood at the end of the bed. He leaned forward and clutched the footboard.

I was visibly breathing hard then. I could feel my chest rising and falling harder and faster the more he stared at me.

He donned a dark-coloured shirt and what appeared to be lounge pants. But his easy-going attire didn't mislead me.

I knew how dangerous Billy was whether he was killing in a three- piece suit or sweats and a T-shirt.

"You've been kissing me," I said but it was more to myself. "It was never a dream."

He chuckled low and deep. Humourlessly.

"Sweet, naive girl. You and I both know it wasn't a dream, even if you tried telling yourself that."

He walked to stand before me. I surveyed his body and saw that, although he wore lounge gear, I'd observed a revolver nestled at his side, the metal poking out from beneath his shirt, the violence from it tangible.

He took another stride forward. All I could do was sit there and tip my head back to stare into his torturously lovely face. For long seconds, he didn't speak.

Neither did I.

We merely stared at one other, as if quietly coming to some kind of accord.

"You can always say no," Billy finally said.

I knew what he meant, yet I said nothing.

He smirked and reached out, seized my ponytail, and wrapped it around his wrist. "That's my good girl," he muttered.

And I melted right then upon hearing that praise. It was only four words, but they provoked such a visceral reaction in me that a moan was torn from my throat and spilled out.

Billy took a step back, and I felt an abrupt wave of coldness overtake me. It seemed wrong not having him close.

I questioned my sanity.

"You can always say no," he added again, and although I didn't directly say anything, I shook my head in response. It was a subconscious act but one that had the corner of his mouth grinning.

I knew he wouldn't give me another out. "Then keep being my good girl and show me that little pussy."

Billy

My cock jerked as the words left my mouth and I gave the order for Melissa to do what I wanted. I surely hadn't intended the evening to wind up with me ordering my girl to show me her virgin cunt, but I'd given her the chance to say no.

I wouldn't have liked hearing it, but I would have honored her preferences.

She didn't do what I said immediately. Instead, my darling Melissa stood, her hands visibly quivering as she twisted them in the material of her blouse and approached closer.

I hummed in satisfaction; not even upset she wasn't obeying me promptly. I bent my finger toward her, and she came forward another step. Then one more, until she was standing straight in front of me and the delicious aroma of her innocence filled my nostrils.

She lifted her hand, and I tensed when she placed the tips of her fingers on the center of my chest. Melissa trailed them down, and my abdomen constricted. She let out a gentle breath and slid her fingers over my side, her delicate nails scratching gently over the fabric.

I'd never felt such tremendous fucking pleasure, and she wasn't even touching my bare skin. And for just a second, my eyes closed as I gave in to the sensations.

That's all the time my tiny wildcat needed.

She grabbed my gun and stumbled back.

I didn't rush her, didn't even move. I squinted my eyes and snarled low as she pointed the handgun squarely at me.

Her hands trembled and her expression expressed so much uncertainty.

My cock thickened even more.

I took a step forward, and she shook her head vehemently, moving to the side and away from the bed.

She was rushing toward the bedroom door, but my sweet child wouldn't get far even if she got out. The door stopped her from going any further, and I advanced, my movements languid, lazy even.

Melissa lifted her arms and clasped her fists securely around the weapon. The gun was now level with my chest.

"Don't come any closer or I'll shoot." Her voice shook as much as her hands did. "I swear to fucking God, Billy, I'll put a bullet right through your heart."

I grinned and reached down, squeezing the gigantic erection I had. It was growing thicker and harder with each passing second.

God she is fucking hot!

I moved forward until I crowded her. The muzzle of the gun now pressed to the center of my chest. I placed one hand beside her head on the door and used my other to curl my fingers around hers, keeping the gun pressed against my body.

She licked her lips, and I fixed my focus on the act, keeping back my groan at the vision of those gorgeous, pink and plump lips wrapped around my cock.

"Caught you off guard," she muttered. "Only reason I got this damn thing." Her voice was a little stronger, a little deeper. Her arousal was coming through.

I groaned at the very thought of her pussy being wet for me, all juicy and ripe for my cock. I leaned forward so the gun jabbed harder into my chest.

Her eyes widened as she glanced down, the worry on her expression apparent enough that I realized she had no plans of shooting me. "You surprised me, you sexy, little vixen." I grinned. "Bet your gorgeous ass has never even shot a gun, let alone held one."

She swung her gaze up to mine before it narrowed slightly. "You don't know shit about me."

Oh, how wrong she was.

"You know that's a lie, Sunshine."

She wet her lips once more. "I've held plenty of guns. You have to know how to conduct yourself when you're nothing and—"

I had a hold of her throat before she even finished getting the words out, my mouth so close to hers that I knew she'd feel my lips move as I spoke. "Never, ever fucking say you're nothing. And certainly not in my fucking presence, Sunshine."

I felt her hold on the gun lessen and, with a twist of my hand, snatched the gun away and held it up between us.

She stared at me, scared, and I couldn't help but breathe out in arousal.

"You've never fucking held a gun in your life." I switched the safety off to illustrate my point.

Her lips pushed together tightly, and I dragged my tongue across them, causing her to cry out in outrage and need.

With the safety still off, I retreated an inch and, while retaining her eyes, trailed my tongue up the barrel and licked the muzzle.

I placed the safety back in place and shoved the gun in the rear waistband of my sweats. And then, I slammed my hand on the door on the other side of her head and crowded the hell out of her.

"Now, lie to me again and tell me your pussy isn't wet right now."

We looked at each other for several seconds in this quiet war of wills.

She wouldn't win, even if I gave her the notion, she had power.

"Go on, Mellie. Lie to me again and tell me your pussy isn't drenched for me."

I didn't make her answer me. The question had been rhetorical. But as her small nostrils flared and her pupils dilated, she demonstrated to me she was ready for me even if she fucking despised it.

"I'm only going to say this once more." I took another step back. "You can say no, but if you're not going to, get that pretty ass on the bed and give me what I fucking want, Melissa."

I gave her only a moment to pick her route, but she didn't make me wait. Melissa shuddered and walked her sexy ass to the bed.

And I watched her, wishing this moment was in slow motion. She gave in so nicely.

Melissa got back into the bed and laid down. She softly spread her legs.

I grasped my cock. The length had been thick before she'd even woken up.

I'd been so hard as I watched her sleep, as I stroked her gorgeous pink lips with my tongue until she parted them a little for me.

I'd let that muscle go over her face, past her cheekbones, and to the tip of her nose.

She smelt so sweet and clean, like the soap I'd bought particularly for Melissa. Everything in here, I'd hand-picked, wanting her to use the things I bought and wear the clothing I selected.

She looked so gorgeous lying on my bed with those huge dark eyes and that worried look on her face.

"Spread your legs and make sure they're wide."

They said males were a visual species, but I wasn't hard because I stared at Melissa half-dressed with her legs open as far as they could go. My balls weren't drawn up tight since her small panties were somewhat wedged up her slit, showing me a prime sight of her pussy lips and the damp spot right in the heart of that cloth.

I wasn't even this aroused because I was about to fuck Melissa, yet I was. Although, that was a huge part of why my cock throbbed. The truth of the matter was, my cock was stiffer than a fucking lead pipe because I knew she'd be mine in every conceivable way.

I was turned on more than I'd ever been in my God forsaken life. I knew she was a little anxious about being with me… concerned about the pain, that I'd damage her. And I will, but not in the way she feared. I wanted her suffering to be filled with pleasure.

I laid the handgun aside and slipped out of my pants but left my briefs on. I wanted her to see how the fabric obscenely tented in front from how hard and large my cock was.

Because of her.

"You see what you do to me?" I grabbed my erection and fisted it. "You gorgeous, little fucking tease."

She was so little compared to me, all slim, feminine curves and pert little breasts that had my tongue thick and my mouth watering.

The first few times I pushed into her would hurt as her pussy grew acclimated to my dick. I would ease inside her and make her acclimated to my size.

And I anticipated it.

Fuck me, but I looked forward to breaking her in as mine.

Only mine.

Her doubt lit me up from the inside out. But it was her wrath and the way her lovely eyes enlarged when she glanced at me when we passed each other that made me need her like no other.

"I want you to be my whore, Melissa."

Her small nostrils flared, and her gaze furrowed at my words.

I smirked.

Good, let my tiny hellcat be mad. It'll make fucking her all the more pleasure.

"I can see how much you hate me." I bared my teeth. I knew my rage was tangible. I shouldn't care if anyone despised me, and I didn't.

But with her?

Knowing there was this distaste for me even after she lusted after me ticked me the fuck off.

I was on her a second later, my palms flat on each side of her head, my gigantic frame forcing her to spread her legs further to accommodate me.

My cock was so hard that I obscenely ground it between her thighs.

She gasped.

"And that's okay." I leaned down and slid my nose up the side of her throat, inhaling. Scenting her. "Because I'm going to fuck it out of you." I leaned in close, my lips near her ear, and murmured, "I'm never letting you go. Not of your own accord. And sure as hell not by someone else's hand."

I seized her chin, leaned back, and forced my mouth down on hers, sealing those words against her because both of our lives depended on them.

"Now tell me what the fuck I want to hear, you beautiful girl." I peered into her eyes and grabbed her chin so she couldn't look away. I knew she wanted to. She was afraid right now and not simply of what I had planned for her but more so because she wanted this.

I could smell how wet her little cunt was for me, and had seen how juicy she had gotten.

My gorgeous fucking whore was primed.

"I hate you," she eventually murmured, and I chuckled. "But…" she inhaled hard and exhaled gently. "God help me… I want this."

I grinned at her, and no doubt, I looked like the predator I was. "You're not going to turn me down, are you, Melissa?"

Snowed in with the Mafia

She didn't vocally answer, but shook her head.

"You're going to give me whatever I want, isn't that right." I didn't phrase it like a question.

She licked those exquisitely plump pink lips and nodded.

"Yes, sir, anything."

Billy

HER REMARK MADE me snarl with ecstasy. I could admit when I'd met my match. I was growing weak where Melissa was concerned. I'd already murdered for her.

Easily.

Without consideration.

And I'd do it again and again.

The only thing that could pull her apart from me was if I fucking died. "Mmm, you please me like no one else ever has. You make me feel things, sweetheart." I leaned in and dragged my tongue over the side of her face. "How badly do you want me to fuck you?" I whispered against her ear.

She groaned, "God, I want that." She lifted her hips, trying to rub her small pussy on my throbbing cock.

I needed her free of all her garments. The fact she was hardly clad turned me on, but god, I wanted to see her bare.

I tore away our remaining pieces, enraged at the fabric for keeping her from me.

Fuck, my dick ached. "Yeah," I gasped at the pleasure and anguish, at the vision of her naked and quivering beneath me. "Yeah, I know you want me to fuck you. You want me to make it hurt, don't you?"

She whimpered and grasped my biceps, pushing her claws into my flesh.

I was walking on a wire, my body feeling stiff, my cock aching. Pre-cum was leaking out the tip of my shaft, and all I could think about was dragging the crown over her pussy and putting my fragrance all over her.

I ran my tongue over her bottom lip, and she shivered for me. "You want me to make that tight, little pussy sore?"

I knew she was seconds away from splintering for me, so I pushed her harder. I wanted her out of her comfort zone so all she did was let me handle the scenario and make her come apart.

She didn't react, but I didn't encourage her to use her words. She'd be screaming my name soon enough.

I stepped away from her, and she made the loveliest, most vulnerable sound. I grasped my shaft and stroked myself, squeezing out pre-cum and staring in rapt delight as it spilled over her tummy.

She gasped.

My actions were rapid because I didn't want her apprehension to overshadow what I was going to have her do. I had a knee on either side of her stomach, my much bigger physique making her look little beneath me.

I had a hand squeezing my cock, and the way she closed her eyes and inhaled nearly had me coming.

But I wanted her looking at me when I slammed my fat cock into her throat. I softly grasped her chin with my thumb and tipped her head back.

"Look at me, Melissa."

My body tightened further as she did what I said without hesitation.

For several moments, neither of us talked. I kept her chin between my fingers and rubbed my dick while I let my gaze travel over her breasts.

My pre-cum was making a sticky mess all over her neck and upper chest, but that's precisely what I fucking wanted.

"Rub my cum into your body." I let go of her chin and slowly stroked my finger across her jawline, along her face, and to her mouth. "Don't make me tell you again."

Snowed in with the Mafia

She lifted her arm and ran her fingers over her throat, over the little indent at the hollow, and over her breasts. I didn't have to tell her to rub my cum into her breasts. She did that all on her own.

I held my breath and just watched. The sight of what she was doing was very appealing. "Now suck on your fingers, Melissa. Lick them clean."

God, I'd never seen anything hotter than this female right here.

I leaned in so our faces were so near. When she performed what I asked, I could hear the wet noises of her tongue gliding over her fingers.

"Tell me how I taste."

Her eyes fluttered closed, and she murmured. "Like power."

My cock was harder than hell still, thick and long, proud, and eager to fuck the hell out of her.

"Such a good girl," I hummed low.

While watching her lick her fingers, I reached out and touched her drenched pussy. She was slick, her cunt so ready for me that there would be little resistance when I finally fucked her. She was tight, my tiny virgin, and it would hurt no matter what, but I'd break her in so her body got acclimated to my size.

I stroked her clit, and she elevated her hips. Melissa was ready for my cock, and I was barely hanging on. But I liked prolonging the pleasure. I fucking loved the edge of waiting out an orgasm.

After rubbing that tiny bud a few times, I moved down and braced my hands on either side of her head and leaned in, replacing her digits with my mouth and tongue.

"Open wider for me," I urged against her mouth.

She parted her lips and did what I said. I plunged my tongue inside, and she moaned. I grunted from our combination of flavors.

I tunneled my fingers through her hair, and I knew it hurt

because of her gasp. But I didn't loosen my hold. Instead, I tightened it, which had her moaning this time.

With each passing second, I felt my hold on her became more forceful, my kiss more demanding.

We did this for far too long. I'd rather be fucking her, but I couldn't stop kissing her, didn't want to stop hearing the sexy sounds that left her.

She was liquid for me.

I finally forced myself to pull back and sucked in a lungful of air. "So sweet," I murmured as I stared down at her. I dragged my tongue over her top lip then the bottom one, lapping at her repeatedly, slowly, languidly. Like a lion grooming his female.

And then, I dragged my tongue along her jawline and moved it lower until I was sucking at the pulse point right below her ear.

"You'll be my good girl and do what I say, isn't that right?" I was torturing Melissa. I knew that. She could barely breathe easily because her arousal was too intense. "Use your words, you beautiful, fucking girl."

She finally whispered, "Yes."

I groaned.

Jesus Christ.

I'd never wanted anything more in my life than I did Melissa.

With one more long, lazy lick along the side of her throat, I pulled back, gripped my cock again, and looked into her eyes.

"Watch me as I jerk off."

Her gaze dropped to do just that.

"You see how hard you make me?" I stroked myself. "You see how big and hard you make my cock?"

She nodded and parted her mouth.

"You're watching my cock like you're hungry for it." I bared my teeth as pleasure shot up my spine. "You want a taste right from the fucking source?" I didn't expect a verbal answer. Her primed body and the way she gyrated her hips were answer enough.

She lifted her hands and placed them on my thighs before rising slightly.

"Open for me, Melissa."

Her lips parted, and I moved closer and up to straddle her shoulders with my cock in hand. She curled her fingers against my thighs, digging her nails into my skin until I hissed. That pain felt so fucking good.

She leaned forward without me giving her direction. Her eyes closed as she dragged her tongue around the crown.

"Look at me," I snarled. I gripped her jaw, prying her mouth open, and while staring into her eyes, I let a trail of saliva fall from my mouth and into hers.

Her eyes got wide, my darling, tiny virgin. It was such a turn on she was so inexperienced.

No one will have her but me.

Fucking never.

I let one more trail of saliva drip into her mouth, and for just a second, it was still connected to my lips as it reached her tongue. And like my good girl, Melissa swallowed.

I groaned.

She closed her eyes again, and I yelled sharply, "No, you watch me." She quickly opened her eyes, and I hummed. "Now, open wider because I'm going to fuck your throat." She let her jaw relax, and I heard it pop. I didn't know why that sound aroused me like it did, but my balls drew up tight with my impending climax.

I slipped in deeper till the tip of my dick met the back of her throat. A guttural, even savage, sound left me with emotion. "I want to hear you gag." I drew out and thrust back in several times, fucking her mouth a bit deeper with each stroke. Her eyes were watering, and every time I pushed all the way back, she gagged for me.

"Christ," I swore between my teeth. "Look at how pretty you look stuffed full of my dick." I fucked her between her lips nice and slow. "You're so fucking beautiful. So sexy."

I let my eyes close then, savoring the feeling of her throat tightening around my cockhead every time I drove in deep. But keeping them closed didn't last long because I wanted to see her suck me off too damn badly.

"I've never felt anything so fucking good before." I grabbed her hair and started dragging her forward as I thrust back in, using her face to fuck myself. "Be my good girl and make me come, Melissa." Spit trickled from the corners of her mouth. "Fuck, that's hot."

Her cheeks were wet as she continually gagged on my cock, but she never once glanced away from me. She tried to push me away with her hands on my thighs, but I snarled like an animal refusing to give up his meat. I bared my teeth as I dragged her face toward me, demanding her continue to suck my dick.

"Breathe… through your nose." The words were broken. I utilized her for my pleasure.

And she let me.

"You're going to make me come, Sunshine. You're making me feel so damn good, baby, as I watch you drink me up." I growled low and tightened my fingers in her hair so hard a strangled sound left her. "Look at how pretty you are with your lips stretched wide and wrapped around my cock. Fuck," I cursed. "You're going to make me come harder than I ever have. Swallow every drop, Melissa. Don't make me punish you for wasting any."

My whole body felt rigid, my lips pushed back from my teeth. "Fuck. Here I come."

With one thrust.

Two.

And on the third one, I buried my dick deep in the back of her throat and came.

Her eyes widened as my seed flew right down her throat. She didn't even have to fucking swallow.

I eventually relaxed, my thrusting becoming gentle and sluggish. "God damn."

I withdrew out, and she inhaled roughly before blowing it out

slowly. Her lips were so lovely, so pink and puffy from giving me head.

I stroked a finger over her lower lip, leaned in, and murmured, "Now I'm going to get my girl off."

Melissa

"Now, I'm going to get my girl off."

I replayed that phrase repeatedly until I felt euphoric from them. My jaw ached, my throat was sore, and the flavor of his cum coated my entire mouth. But I'd never felt more excited in my entire life as I glanced up at Billy. He carried this dangerous look on his face that made me feel like molten lava.

Billy rolled off of me, laid down on his back, and grabbed my waist. He repositioned me so I straddled his waist; my pussy was so moist I felt how sticky my inner thighs were.

When Billy gripped my hips painfully, I closed my eyes and moaned at how much the sting of pressure and suffering felt so damn nice.

He leaned forward and stroked the tip of his nose over my throat before licking. I heard and felt his buzz of animalistic joy.

"Rub that primed, soaked, little pussy back and forth on my cock. Work that cunt against me like you're anxious to come."

Billy bit down on my neck firmly.

My inside muscles tensed, and I started moving against him, working myself over and using him.

God that was heated.

I slowly rolled my hips, moving them in a circle, Billy's hands guiding me. His cock was trapped between my pussy lips as I established a perfect rhythm that sent shock waves through me.

The more I rotated my hips, the greater my enjoyment climbed. I sought it until I knew euphoria was right at my fingertips.

My head rolled backwards, too heavy to hold up, and I closed my eyes as I just gave in to the agony.

"That's it. Be Daddy's good girl and come for me." His use of the word Daddy should not have set off fireworks in me. But I yelled out as I came, that lone word paired with his praise sending me over the edge.

Everything faded as I exploded, my motions jerking as I gave way to the sensations. The orgasm seemed to go on and on, and only as consciousness came flooding back to me did I take a large lungful of air.

Billy whispered something; words that sounded gentler than anything I'd ever heard him speak before.

I fell forward and felt the lightest touch as he caressed my back. Despite him coming down my throat, he was still rock hard and writhing between my pussy lips.

I could have fallen asleep just like that, laying over his chest with his massive hands sliding up and down my back. My body felt heavier as sleep seized me, but the heavy rumble of Billy speaking awakened me.

"Sweet girl... You don't think I'm done with you yet, do you?" He grinned like a shark. "Come up here and sit on my face. I don't want to be able to breathe because your pussy is drowning me."

I licked my lips, my mouth suddenly dry, my neck constricted even though he'd showered it with thick jets of his come.

"So wet from your orgasm, baby. I want my mouth covered with it."

His hands on my waist were terrible and severe, and I wanted marks covering me, wanted to look in the mirror and see the little purple and blue fingerprints left behind by this meeting.

"Do as I said."

I pressed my fingers into his big shoulders until he hissed and moved up the bed. My heart was thumping so hard and fast it was hurting.

"Brava bambina."

He smacked my ass hard enough the skin jiggled, and a little sound escaped me.

"Bring that pretty pussy here."

He spanked my ass again and roared in approval when I obeyed.

He stared at me between the legs for a bit before he spit on my slit. I gasped at the feet of his saliva on my pussy, then the sensation of it sliding down my crevice.

"So pretty."

He dragged his tongue from vaginal hole to clit.

My hands instantly flew to his hair, and I gripped on as Billy licked through my pussy, teasing my hole, and then flattened that muscle to move it back up to my clit. He did this repeatedly, gently nipping my lips while he held me open with his thumbs and forefingers.

He made these terrible, animalistic sounds while he was unrelenting between my thighs.

"I want you to come for me. Be my nasty, good girl and give Daddy what he wants, and then I'll fuck you." He sucked my clit into the warm, wet recesses of his mouth, and I let my head fall back.

I brazenly massaged my pussy back and forth, feeling my climax swell.

I came again, this time the pleasure was so rapid and strong I couldn't even breathe through it. When I relaxed, Billy grabbed my hips, tossing me onto my back.

All he did was stare at my naked body. My legs felt like

rubber and were splayed, extended so wide I felt my inner lips opening for his vision.

He ran a palm across his mouth, groaning deep within his throat.

"Look at you," Billy whispered in a voice so low I knew those words weren't for me. He stroked his free hand up my inner thigh, but that's where the tenderness ended. While peering into my eyes, he brought his palm down on my bare, sensitive pussy and spanked me.

I shouted out and tried to seal my legs, but he smacked my pussy again. "Keep yourself open for me. I want to see how red and swollen I can make this gorgeous cunt."

When he paddled my pussy a third time, I felt the anguish evolve into a deeper, darker pleasure. Maybe he realized the effect it had on me because he mumbled out, "Jesus," and squeezed my clit between his thumb and forefinger.

And then with a delicious curse, Billy covered my body with his, grasped my throat, and kissed me like he owned me.

I was already prepared and ready as he used his body to force my legs open, used his free hand to curl his fingers into my inner thigh, and glide the digits to the center of my body.

My eyes widened on their own when I felt the tip of his hot, thick cockhead at my entry.

Billy drew back and gazed into my eyes.

"Any other man would take your virginity sweet. Slow." He licked the side of my cheek, humming. "But I'm the bad guy, so you get it how I like it, Sunshine." And with that, he pushed his cock into me so hard that my back slid up the mattress.

I had to reach up and over my head to support my hand on the headboard to stop myself from moving any more… to absorb all his firm, thick length.

I closed my eyes as the intense sting of pain from him breaking through my innocence crashed into me. It stole my breath and made me feel foggy. The fullness and stretch was like nothing I'd ever be able to describe.

The snarl that came out of him as he plunged himself deep inside my body had me snapping my eyes back wide.

"No, beautiful girl. Keep those wonderful eyes on me." Billy kept his pacing slow and easy at first, and a part of me wanted to taunt him about the big talk he just gave me about being the bad guy.

I wasn't a fool in thinking he wasn't the anti-hero of his own story, but he'd been laying me breadcrumbs of sweetness that made me wonder if there wasn't as much evil in him as he wanted me to believe.

Maybe it was the way my face relaxed as I stroked my hands up his massive biceps that tipped him off to where my thoughts were. Because darkness passed across his face and he chuckled quietly. He leaned in so his mouth was at my ear.

"I think my little virgin assumes I'm not the monster I really am." He pulled back and leaned on his knees, holding my thighs open with his hands.

"My good, fucking girl." His hand curled around my jaw. "Open for me." He added pressure until I did just that.

I wasn't sure what his plans were, but I didn't anticipate him to lean forward and slowly let a trail of saliva descend from his tongue and trickle into my mouth.

His spit was warm and tasted just like Billy, spicy and macho and everything else I couldn't put into words. But instinct had me trying to turn my head. His fingers on my jaw kept me in place as he let another long, thick trail of saliva fall across my lips.

This should have been horrible, fucking nasty to let him spit in my mouth like this.

Then why am I getting turned on all over again?

He started pulling out and pushing back in, fucking me as he let saliva drop out of his lips and spill across my throat, my breasts, using his other hand to rub it all in.

He tunneled his cock in and out of me, tongue sweeping, teeth biting, never stopping.

I was immersed in the feelings as I curled my hands around his powerfully muscled arms.

Billy looked so savage right now, primeval in his hunger, panting. And the entire time, he never stopped fucking me.

"God, you're fucking hot. The hottest thing I've ever seen."

A howl of pain and delight poured from my throat as he crashed into me, each thrust harder than the last.

"I'm about to blow my load at the very sight of you covered in my spit."

He peered at where we were joined, watching as he fiercely claimed me.

"This virgin pussy is all swollen and red, stretched so wide around my dick. Popping your little cherry has my cock all splattered with blood, Sunshine."

He placed his thumb on my clit, but I didn't think I could come again, not with the soreness still there and having gotten off already.

"That's alright, sweet girl," he responded as if he knew what I was thinking. "Once I've broken this pussy in just for me, I'll make sure you get off a minimum of three times a night."

I tipped my head back, closed my eyes, his words a powerful aphrodisiac. I could feel his cock thicken even further inside of me. And when he cursed and filled me as he came, I swore I could feel the thick, hot, and milky jets of his cum pouring out and covering every inch of my insides.

I didn't know how long he stayed inside of me, but I could tell by his expression his climax was long, and it seemed like it lasted forever. When Billy collapsed over me, our breathing was identical as we gasped for air.

It was only after a few short-lived minutes of his cock weakening inside of me that he eventually pulled out.

A sound of disappointment left me. It was one I couldn't have held in. A wave of coldness engulfed my body, and I shuddered involuntarily.

It was the sense of his fingertips gently smoothing down the middle of my body that had me opening my eyes. I wasn't even aware they'd closed.

"So, fucking pretty," he moaned and ran circles around my pussy hole. "It's hot as hell watching my cum slip out of this gorgeous body, but…" he lifted his gaze and peered into my eyes. "I belong deep inside of you."

He thrust two thick fingers in me, driving his sperm back into my body. A loud sound left him.

He shoved those fingers in and out of me till I wriggled beneath him, my body too sore and sensitive. When he put his palm up, it was to show me how shiny and pink-tinged they were.

I licked my lips which Billy took for an invitation. He placed his fingers on my lips.

"Open up and clean my fingers."

I wasn't nearly done sucking on those digits, recognizing how thrilling it was to clean our mingled secretions off them while he watched me.

He slipped out of my mouth and spread his now wet palm over my breasts and belly, as if marking me.

He held my cheek and brushed his thumb over my mouth, tracing my lips. His attitude was so harsh that it was a touch terrifying, and although I knew he wouldn't injure me, I still felt that survival instinct spring up.

"I'm too selfish. You're mine." His voice was pitched low, almost so low that I wondered if I heard him correctly.

I wanted to inquire what he meant, but the heavy hand of sleep was drawing me under and, coupled with the warmth of his body against mine, had a heavy fog claiming me.

Just before the darkness grabbed me, I understood that the

things he spoke meant far more than maybe I was ready to take.

Melissa

ALTHOUGH LAST NIGHT had been great, I kept wondering why I'd caved in.

Why had I been so weak in the face of pleasure?
Why didn't I despise my lack of self-control?

I was furious with myself, but I didn't regret any of it.

I got ready for the day, but my thoughts were entirely filled by Billy. I didn't know if I completely understood what I consented to... this coerced deal.

He'd said I could leave, a part of me knew he wouldn't have merely stood aside. I'd seen that possession in his eyes, that fire burning in the dark depths that had taken my breath away.

He wasn't the prince who would save the day.

He was the devil giving me the deal of a lifetime.

I was selfish, eager to explore these deeper urges and impulses that bewildered me but made me feel more alive than I'd ever felt.

Isn't that why people achieved dangerous feats?
Life-threatening acts?
They wanted to experience that surge to know they were alive.
I wanted that feeling again and again.

And being with Billy was surely like walking over hot coals. I knew the chance of my being burned was inevitable, but I still wanted to see if I won at the end.

When I opened the bedroom door, I figured the guard would be in position, but I was alone. I didn't even see any workers walking the halls.

Of course, he isn't going to need you on lock and key now. You agreed to be his whore.

A shudder passed through me at that notion, and it was one that was totally wonderful.

I wasn't truly alone. There were cameras and possibly guards stationed at all access points.

I headed down the hallway in a thick pair of socks, took the stairs, and when I reached the landing, I heard the clinking of pots and pans in the kitchen.

It was early enough that I knew breakfast would be served at any time.

The simple thought of Billy sitting at the end of the table in the dining room made my pulse beat a little faster.

In excitement?
In anticipation?
God... in arousal?
Yes, to everything of that.

I entered the dining room but was initially surprised to see the table was only set for one.

Me.

A hollowness in the pit of my stomach increased, and I placed my hand on my belly, loathing myself for feeling anything save satisfaction that I would have some space from him.

But all I could think about was how he penetrated me last night and took my virginity.

The splattered blood on the bedding. His cum drying next to it. I started to sweat.

For the next half hour, I ate my breakfast alone; the only sound I could hear was that of the crew in the kitchen cleaning up.

Once completed, I strolled the halls, hoping that I'd run

into him. I sat out in the garden during my lunch an hour later, even had a nap in the solarium after that. My feet were still painful from the prior night's altercation, but I'd been given first aid items to treat them.

And the whole day, I prayed I would see Billy.

But I didn't.

Not after breakfast or after lunch or even when dinner rolled around.

Once again, I felt this strange panic well-up in me. I couldn't place it. I couldn't even describe it if anyone had asked me.

But I loathed it.

It was as the sun was sinking and I finished dinner that I made my way into the library. I cuddled up on the leather settee with a heavy blanket over my lap, a big book in my hands, and the sunset illuminating the vast room in tones of pinks and oranges. But it wasn't long after that when I heard the heavy thump-thump-thump of footsteps coming.

He entered the room. And although I hadn't looked up from the pages, I didn't need to in order to know who it was watching me.

My hands shook as I closed the book, laid it on the tiny coffee table beside me, and finally glanced at Billy.

He stood in the foyer, a three-piece suit on, not hiding how huge and strong he was. Without saying a word, he stepped in, closed the door, and trapped himself in the room with me.

My body instantaneously reacted.

My breathing increased.

My nipples stiffened.

My pussy overflowed.

He said nothing as he strolled to the bar, poured himself a drink and then one for me. It was when he handed me the square glass filled with amber- coloured liquid that I moved. I stretched out, hand shaking, and took the crystal.

Our fingertips brushed, and I felt like I'd touched a live wire just from that brief contact.

And still, he stood there silently, drinking his vodka while he observed me. The first taste of the alcohol burned down my throat. My eyes watered and I coughed, wiping away a droplet that fell out of the corner of my lips.

I was going to throw it aside, only having taken that one drink, when he placed a finger under the glass and tipped it back, forcing me to complete it. Fat tears slid down my cheek as I swallowed it down.

Billy took the glasses, laid them away, and then faced me and started getting undressed.

"You're going to need that booze for what I have planned tonight."

My throat clenched, and I felt my eyes widen. I didn't ask him what he meant, but he didn't make me wonder.

"I'm fucking your ass tonight, Melissa. Gonna claim that cherry, too."

I shook my head before I knew I was doing it, and he smiled then.

But it was rough, awful. Like a sociopath coming up with his strategy.

"Get undressed for me, sweetheart." He put his jacket and vest away, and started to loosen his tie.

I wanted to argue, to say there was no way I was letting him fuck my ass. It seemed inappropriate on so many levels. But a curiosity took me, and I was rising, the blanket spilling to the floor as I stood and stripped.

"Turn around, bend over the arm of the settee, and spread your legs. I want to see those lovely and pretty ass cheeks split open."

I licked my lips as he pulled off the remaining of his clothing, stepping out of his boxers and slacks, and stood in front of me with a gigantic hard-on.

Snowed in with the Mafia

With knees that felt like pudding, I turned and bent down, the leather so cold on the bare flesh of my belly, an initial jolt that had me pulling in a short intake.

He had me wait before he approached. And when he ran a hand over the curve of my spine, across one of my ass cheeks, and down the back of my leg, I closed my eyes and gripped the cushion as if it were my lifeline.

But that mild, gentle stroking halted when he used his foot to kick my legs wider apart.

"My pretty girl's inner thighs are so slick." Billy spread my pussy lips apart with two fingers, dispersing the fluid about until I was a shivering, blurry mess for him.

He went away, but before I could get my bearings and check to see what he was doing, Billy was back, spreading my ass cheeks open, and then pouring chilly liquid on my other virgin hole.

"On those little toes, Melissa. Lift that ass to me so I can fuck it." His voice sounded unfamiliar.

I lifted up and chanced a look over my shoulder to see Billy staring at my ass, his cock in his free hand as he stroked himself.

When he stared at me, it was to let out a deep exhale a second before he paddled my ass hard enough the agony was instant.

"Such an obedient, little whore."

A moan was drawn from deep in my throat at the insulting word.

While maintaining my eyes with his, Billy ran his fingers between the cheeks, spreading what I now realized was lubrication across my hole. He rubbed the tip of a digit against the stiffness, and reflexively, my inner muscles clenched.

"Mmm, save that for when my cock is deep inside, baby."

He slipped a finger into my ass, slow and leisurely, observing me the whole while. He didn't have to be gentle, I understood this. He was giving me an opportunity to adjust and get used to this foreign penetration.

He placed another finger with the first, both digits now buried deep and making me feel a strange kind of full.

When he scissored the digits, stretching me to receive his huge dick, I had sweat collecting on the center of my spine.

"Breathe," he mumbled and started thrusting them in and out of me.

Fucking me.

I exhaled; not aware I'd been holding my breath.

For so long, all he did was work me over with his fingers in my ass. I pushed back every time he pulled out.

"Touch your clit. Rub it for me."

He leaned forward, latching his teeth on my nape and biting me hard.

I yelled out, experiencing a spark of joy.

He bit many portions of me, no doubt leaving marks, but driving my desire higher.

I touched myself immediately, pressing my teeth into my bottom lip and gasping at the first touch to that little bead. I was so ready to come and knew it wouldn't take much to throw me over the brink.

"Brava bambina," he purred and removed his fingers, and I felt the bulbous tip of his massive cock lined up with my asshole.

Then he started thrusting into me.

Slow.

Easy.

And after he was buried thoroughly, he stilled.

My inner muscles tensed, and he gasped.

Hand on the back of my neck, he pressed my face into the pillow. I was twisted at such an awkward angle that he could only find purchase by placing his foot squarely beside my head.

He pulled all the way out and pushed back in. The tip of

Snowed in with the Mafia

his dick popped through the tight ring of muscle at the entrance. He took one of my arms and pulled it behind me, keeping it stationed at the small of my back.

The sensation of Billy sliding into my ass and pulling out, adding more lubrication frequently so it was nice and slick and his motions flowing, had my jaw falling slack and my eyes rolling back.

With my free hand, I faltered a few times massaging my clit, these new sensations almost too much for me to bear. But God... I was so near.

The whiskey had since warmed my body and made my head feel fuzzy.

I was happy he gave me time to really adjust, but I knew the instant his control snapped.

He started moving back and forth, and the more he moved, the more his motions became a little tougher, a little faster. He moved his foot off the settee, as if he needed stronger stability to penetrate me like an animal.

My ass tightened around his cock on its own, and Billy groaned, now holding either side of my bottom and keeping the cheeks spread as he fucked me with abandon.

"You're taking my cock in your ass so well, Melissa. I'm going to come so hard, baby."

I forced my eyes open but kept rubbing my clit as I gazed over my shoulder at him.

Billy had his concentration on where he fucked me.

"I could use more lube," he mumbled and glanced at me. "But I'm not going to."

And then he spit between my cheeks, using his saliva as lubricant and thrusting into me.

"It's good, Sunshine. Christ, you feel so fucking nice. So perfect."

I didn't look away as I came closer to my orgasm. Sweat coated his entire body and a few droplets from his temple dripped onto my back.

It was hot as hell.

"Tell me how good it feels."

I moaned and massaged my clit harder. "I'm so close. It's good. So good, Billy."

He hissed and pushed his fingers into my flesh. "Yeah? Then get off for me. Let me feel your ass milking my cock. I'll reward you for being a nice girl by filling you full with my cum."

"Oh. God," I cried out as my orgasm crashed over me. It was never- ending and stole my whole sanity.

"Fuck. That's it. My dirty, fucking girl. My whore." He slammed into me and came. I felt the thickness of his cock become more obvious as he achieved his release.

He filled me up, marking me, totally claiming every part of me until there would be no doubt that I was his.

I knew I could never go back from this.

He'd branded me in the most primitive, elemental way.

Billy pulled out, and I felt his hot seed drip out of my hole. He kept my cheeks open and saw his cum fall out of me and glide along my inner thigh.

My knees shook and I was sweaty. My eyes were too weary to keep open, and sleeping hunched over this piece of furniture sounded like nirvana.

But Billy scooped me up, and I curled my arms around his neck, rested my head on his shoulder, and closed my eyes as he left the library and took the stairs. I didn't need to inquire where he was taking me. I knew we were in his room instantly.

Everything smelled like that dark and luscious perfume that engulfed him.

I didn't object as he placed me in his bed and took a warm, damp rag to my bottom, cleaning me up. I said nothing when he got in behind me. I kept quiet when he covered us with a sheet and pushed my body to his. Back to chest.

I fell asleep, feeling that this was precisely where I was supposed to be.

Snowed in with the Mafia

Beside Billy.
His hand wrapped around my throat.
Using me.
Knowing he wouldn't allow anyone to hurt me.
Ever.

Billy

I couldn't keep her.

I knew it as soon as I glanced at her gorgeous sleeping figure.

I'd just fucked her three times before I left her fall asleep. Poor girl was no doubt pained from my need for her, but I couldn't control the obsession that raced in my veins.

I had to have her.

Every single part of her.

Every moment of every day.

I'd told myself she was mine, that I couldn't, wouldn't let her go. But with each passing moment, I knew that was the biggest damn lie I'd ever told myself.

She was a vulnerability to me.

My only weakness, and I wasn't about to let some fucking chick hold my heart in her palm.

But I couldn't take my eyes off of her.

I kept seeing myself getting in behind Melissa and holding her all night. I'd carry a gun in one hand as I made sure she was protected.

But I pushed myself to leave and proceeded into my study where I spotted Robert waiting for me.

He sat in front of my desk, a bourbon in one hand, and his other arm hung over the back of the chair. He said nothing, and neither did I, as I poured myself a drink, sat behind my desk, and stared at him.

"You're in too deep," he finally replied and then took a long drink from his glass.

I clenched my jaw. I knew exactly what, or should I say who, he was referring to.

Melissa.

"Mind your fucking business," was all I said.

His own jaw tightened. And although I knew he wanted to retaliate, since he was the same type of man I was, he recognized his place.

He was loyal.

He kept his lips shut and followed directions.

"And, yeah. I fucking know I am." I leaned back and scrubbed a hand over my face, having not shaved in days, hearing and feeling the scruff on my cheeks and jaw.

But she'd told me how much she'd liked it one night after I'd teased her.

So, I kept it. And I'd eaten her, knowing that I was grinding my cheeks against her inner thighs, the whiskers adding a little of discomfort that made her come even harder.

My cock thickened at the very concept.

"What are your plans?"

Robert didn't have to expand for me to understand what he was talking about.

Everything that has to do with Melissa.

Her being here, keeping her, and not wanting to let her go.

I recognized the reality of the situation. She was my vulnerability, my only one. The one weakness I'd ever had in my godforsaken existence.

Oh, I already knew the answer to Robert's inquiry. But I stayed mute, tossing it around in my thoughts constantly.

"She'd be a target." Robert was staring into his glass, zero emotion on his face.

I was quite confident the fucker was a sociopath. He never demonstrated empathy. He'd always been a cold-blooded killer. Just like me.

"They'd use her to get to you."

Again, this was just trash that I replayed in my thoughts.

"I see the way you look at her." Robert stared at me, his eyes such a light blue that were nearly translucent. "She's too good for you."

That was an irrefutable fact.

"And I know you're a selfish man when it comes to what you want, but…" He leaned forward, supporting his elbows on his thighs. "I want you to think long and hard about if your enemies got a hold of her. What they'd do to her… how they'd take out their hatred for you on her."

I felt a burning in my veins at the very concept. I wanted to rush over to the table and slice Robert's throat for even bringing that up. I realized what he was doing, how he was trying to make me see reality. He knew there was a small bit of doubt, and he was scared I wouldn't make what he felt was the right option.

I gritted.

"Fucking watch, it."

I might not kill the guy, but I'd beat the snot out of him just for saying her name.

"Just pointing out the obvious." He leaned back, finished his glass, and laid it down. "If it hurts this bad at just the hypothetical thought of it…" He stopped, as if trying to really let the fucking words sink in.

I snarled at him.

"Then think of the kind of pain you'll feel if it's made a reality."

I knew what I wanted to do and what I should do. And those two things were at battle. It was a fight to the bleeding death, fists crashing into flesh, weapons pulling out pieces.

I'd always been a greedy motherfucker, had always just gone after what I wanted. I'd never thought anything of it, never envisaged my existence where I didn't gain every fucking thing I desired.

But with Melissa… it was different.

Because I'd had nothing, I cared about losing.

She was different.

She made me feel different, feel more… alive and hopeful.

She was that sliver of light, the only thing that could penetrate the darkest portion of my psyche.

So, when I looked at Robert, I knew precisely what I had to do. And I had to convince myself it's what I wanted.

This decision wasn't for me.

It was for her.

To safeguard my girl.

Because making sure she was safe was the only thing I fucking cared about.

I finished my drink and remarked in a voice that was stern, unyielding, and one I used for everyone around me, "I'm going to let her go after the two weeks are up because she doesn't belong here."

Melissa

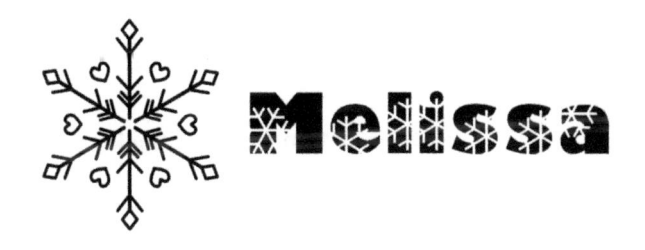

FOR THE NEXT TWO WEEKS, the sex with Billy was constant.

Intense.

He introduced me to sexual experiences I didn't even realize were possible.

My body was covered in minor bruises from his tight grips. The impressions of his teeth damaged the sides of my neck.

I couldn't help but feel they were a symbol of ownership. I glanced at them in the mirror and ran my fingertips over them.

And the closer it got to the end of our pact, the stranger I felt. I couldn't articulate what exactly it was, but it filled my thoughts day and night.

With each passing day, I was caught up further in his web. And a part of me knew he felt the same. The way he looked at me, especially when I caught him off guard, or when he didn't realize I was observing.

The way he touched me... as if he were terrified I'd be snatched away from him.

And then there were the murmured things he said in my ear shortly before I fell asleep. I never understood what he said, the lines in Italian, but they sounded proprietary, as if they sealed that moment in time.

And here I was, at the very end of those fourteen days, I felt anxiety claim me in a chokehold.

My time here was over and I knew I wouldn't go down without a fight.

I wanted Billy and I would tell him just that.

Today.

On the day I was to go and never look back.

Robert, the huge and strong gentleman, who I learnt was Billy's most trusted soldier in his underground army, had come and gotten me.

We said nothing to each other as I was escorted into the library. The significance of this space—where Billy had raped my ass for the first time—wasn't lost on me. I knew it wasn't an accident Billy wanted me here.

Robert departed and slammed the door behind him, and I paced around anxiously. I finally sat on one of the overstuffed seats and bounced my leg, staring at the door and willing it to open so I could get this over with.

And after what felt like a lifetime, the door opened and Billy walked inside.

He strolled immediately to the bar and poured himself a glass, but I didn't miss how he wavered slightly and had to support himself with a hand on the wall.

Brows knitted, I murmured, "Billy?"

Billy's shoulders tensed. But he didn't glance at me, not until a whole minute had passed.

"I think we should talk." I just got right into it. "I want to talk about this… us."

"There is no us," he said immediately.

That hurt significantly stronger than I anticipated it would.

"Will you please look at me?" My voice shook, and I didn't even try to hide it. "Please."

God, why did I have to sound so desperate?

Because I've fallen in love with him, that's why.

He turned around after he threw back a shot. The first thing I noticed was how drunk he truly was. His eyes were glossy and red-rimmed. He crossed his thick arms over his wide chest and stared at me.

"What do you want to talk about?" He cocked one of his eyebrows. He sounded so bored, so irritated with me.

"I want to talk about us," I whispered.

"Stupid girl," he snarled. "Still thinking there was anything more between us than hardcore fucking."

I didn't let his words sink deep enough to hurt or at least that's what I told myself. But it was inevitable. I opened my mouth, but no words came through, lodged in my throat because I felt this tightening in my chest.

He chuckled. "Oh, you poor, little thing. Did you think I wanted anything more from you than your pussy?" He tsked. "I felt nothing for you aside from the moments I was buried deep in your cunt and blowing my load into your body. After that… you were nothing to me once more."

His dark, apathetic expression made everything in me hurt.

"It doesn't seem like you felt nothing for me." I regretted the words after I uttered them because I knew his response would be even more hurtful. "Just like that?"

He grinned. "Just like that."

I hated that my eyes were watering.

Fuck him.

Fuck these feelings.

All of this was nothing but an illusion.

"I'll remind you I paid for these two weeks. You were nothing but my whore."

My rage replaced the hurt, and I narrowed my eyes.

"So, you'll leave today. The snow has melted enough that you'll be fine. All the account information will be handed to you, and Robert will transport you wherever you wish to go."

"You're absolutely right." I straightened my shoulders and elevated my chin. I stood and whispered in a quiet voice,

"Fuck you, Billy. Glad I won't have to see you again for the rest of my life."

Before I could break down and cry, I left the library and rushed to my room, but before I could get there, I heard the library door open and slam shut.

I only made it a handful of feet before I heard the heavy fall of footsteps approaching, and then someone grabbed my arm and whirled me around.

Billy stood right in front of me, his nostrils flaring as he inhaled and exhaled violently. "Don't you fucking walk away from me, Melissa."

I felt my wrath rushing to the surface. "Fuck. You."

He banged his hands against the wall on either side of my head. "Watch it, little girl, or I'll show you a side of myself I reserve for people I hate."

There it was. The minute amount of truth he fought so hard to hide. And by the way his eyes flickered, I knew he understood his deadly blunder. But I was sick of this stuff. If he wanted to push me away, then I'd push right back.

"You're not going to talk to me that way either, asshole. Like you said…" I rose on my toes, still not even nose-to-nose with him because of his imposing height. "I was just your whore. I'm free to go with an account full of your fucking money. So, leave me the hell alone and back the hell up." I placed my hands on his chest and pushed, but he was like steel in front of me.

"Fucking brat. I should spank your ass and leave pretty bruises." He dropped his eyes to stare at my mouth.

"Don't fucking threaten me, Billy." I shoved a finger against the hard wall of his chest.

The corner of his mouth lifted. "I'm not threatening you, Sunshine. I'm telling you the cold, hard truth. If you knew the kind of man I was, you would never have agreed to stay with me and never have agreed to let me in your body."

I clenched my jaw. "You must think I'm a fucking moron. I

know exactly what type of man you are… the type to kill my father and brother because they hurt me repeatedly."

"You think you know me, but you only know the stories the streets tell. The rumors that are layered and that are only half of my reality. The truth is much worse. Darker." He leaned in, all that heat gone, and in its place came something more deviant. "You want to know me, Melissa? The real me?"

His comments were a warning.

"I've killed so many people, I couldn't even tell you a number."

I wasn't surprised but said nothing.

"Growing up, I was nothing but a thief. A criminal. I had to be in order to survive. I did whatever it took to not let the world eat me up. Petty crimes, assault… murder. It got to the point I relished doing it all." His grin was slow, as if thinking about it turned him on. "I wasn't going to let anyone stand in my way. I wasn't going to let anyone have control over me." He held his arms out, his face becoming a monstrous mask.

I didn't know what to say, how to react. He seemed more threatening at this moment than I'd ever seen him.

He felt… cold.

"I could tell you about my shitty childhood and all the heinous shit done to me."

He took a step back, and I got the sensation he didn't fully trust himself around me right now.

"I could go into great detail on all the disgusting and vile things I had to do to stay alive."

Something sinister crossed his face.

"But I'm not going to do any of that. Those are my scars to carry, and frankly, it's not shit I want to hash out with a woman I'd been fucking for the last couple of weeks."

I realized I was crying before I knew it happened. I wasn't upset or terrified. I had no idea why this dam in me had burst. It felt final, though, like this was the last straw to break everything wide open.

"I sell guns, drugs… hell, pussy for a living. I run underground fight rings… ones that finish in death. Did you know I bury bodies outside of town where no one will ever find them?"

He scrubbed a hand over his face, almost looking weary.

"I could have my men get rid of the bodies, but I fucking like doing it, Melissa. I relish burying them into an unmarked grave and covering their rotting corpses with dirt."

I curled my hands into tight fists. He was pushing me away, attempting to intimidate me.

It was working.

"That's it," he purred. "You see the monster I am? Be fucking afraid."

He smashed a fist on his chest.

Repeatedly.

"I'm not capable of caring about someone." His rage seethed. "And I never will. You know why? Because it's not what I fucking want."

I had no one to blame but myself for how I felt, for allowing my heart to open up and feel things for this man.

This monster.

I knew from the very beginning Billy would harm me. I just didn't realize the type of suffering would be from a broken heart.

He stood back, allowing me to leave.

I was frozen for long seconds, just staring at him and knowing this would be the last time I looked into his dark, tumultuous eyes.

"Leave, Melissa." He took another step back. When I didn't move, he yelled, "Get the fuck out of my house!"

His frigid words had me going, stumbling over my feet. All I cared about was getting the hell out of here and never looking back.

Billy

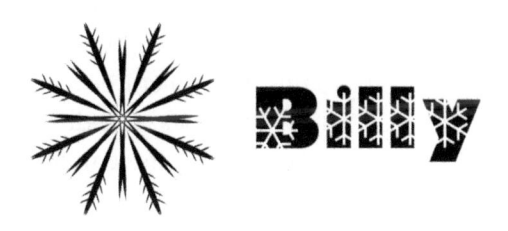

THE WEIGHT of her departure lingered in the air, a heavy, oppressive presence that seemed to seep into the very walls of my office. The door stood closed, a barrier between me and the reality of her absence. I remained ensconced in the dimly lit room, the solitude amplifying the echoes of her footsteps fading away down the corridor.

The silence that settled in the wake of her departure was a haunting reminder of the void she left behind. The house, once vibrant with the warmth of shared moments, now stood desolate, its rooms echoing with a cold, lifeless emptiness. It mirrored the desolation I felt within, a reflection of the void that had swallowed my once-vibrant heart.

Closing my eyes, I exhaled, attempting to release the tension that gripped every fiber of my being. My hands found solace on the worn surface of the desk, fingers digging into the wood as if seeking an anchor in the storm of emotions raging within me.

Abandoning the formality of a glass, I reached for a bottle of bourbon, its amber contents promising a temporary escape from the harsh reality of the present. The clock on the wall seemed to tick with a mocking indifference, counting down the moments of a life unraveled.

The unraveling had not followed the script I had envisioned, but the chaos of it all resonated with a perverse satisfaction within me. It was a satisfaction born out of a twisted desire for her to despise me, to harbor a loathing so profound that it echoed the deadness within my own heart. I welcomed the venomous disdain, believing it to be a fitting punishment for the sins that had led us to this dark juncture.

My eyes remained fixed on the clock as I dialed Robert, the resonance of each ring punctuating the emptiness of the room.

His voice, gravelly and unyielding, answered on the first ring.

"Sí."

"You have her?"

"Sí."

The confirmation was accompanied by a terse acknowledgment of her tears, a confirmation that tightened an invisible noose around my already constricted heart.

"It needed to be this way," I muttered.

Silence met my statement, and I knew no words were necessary. I disconnected the call, resisting the urge to hurl the phone against the unforgiving walls. Instead, I placed it beside me on the couch and lifted the bottle to my lips, the fiery liquid offering a temporary reprieve from the storm raging within.

The bourbon burned its way down my throat, a searing reminder of the chaos I had unleashed. Melissa, a name that once held the promise of love and solace, now echoed with the resonance of regret and shattered dreams. I traced the label on the bottle, my mind drifting to the certainty that, no matter where she sought refuge, I would find her.

Yet, the irony struck me.

The contradiction of my actions - pushing her away only to pursue her - was not lost on me. I hadn't severed ties with her to engage in a futile pursuit. No, my intentions were far more insidious. I craved the agony of watching her slip away, the anguish of knowing I had orchestrated her descent into the abyss.

Snowed in with the Mafia

The unknown agony, a monstrous entity, took residence in the center of my chest, a malevolent force that fueled my anger. The bottle was drained, and I stumbled towards the bedroom, the darkness within mirroring the shadows that danced on the periphery of my soul.

In the quiet of the room, I inhaled deeply, my senses assaulted by the lingering fragrance of Melissa's perfume. The blankets, a sanctuary for the memories we had woven together, now served as a painful reminder of what I had forfeited. I brought them closer, burying my face in the fabric, desperately seeking solace in the traces of her essence that lingered.

Oblivion remained elusive as I grappled with the regret that clawed at the edges of consciousness. I should have gone after her, pursued her with relentless determination. Instead, I had cast her aside, a callous act that branded me as the motherfucker I had become.

She, the only pure thing in my tumultuous existence, had slipped through my fingers. I had discarded her to keep her safe, a paradoxical decision that now haunted the recesses of my guilt-ridden mind. In the quiet of the night, I closed my eyes, conjuring an image of her, still present in the twisted tapestry of my fantasies.

There she was, a phantom of desire, wrapped in the blankets that had witnessed our moments of intimacy. The fantasy unfurled in my mind's eye, a tormented reverie where my hand rested on her throat, where the echoes of our passion lingered in the air, and where the darkness concealed the sins that had driven us apart.

The lines between reality and fantasy blurred, and I clung to the illusions, seeking refuge in the fragments of a love that had crumbled beneath the weight of my own demons. The bourbon-soaked haze enveloped me, and I surrendered to the relentless pull of unconsciousness, a temporary respite from the torment of a heart that beat in sync with the echoes of a love lost.

In the cocoon of darkness, I lay adrift in a sea of regret, the remnants of bourbon-induced warmth fading into a chill that mirrored the cold reality outside.

The bed cradled my form, a solitary figure entangled in the sheets, haunted by the specter of decisions that had unraveled the tapestry of love.

As sleep threatened to claim me, the room became a canvas for memories, each one a brushstroke of passion, pain, and the irreparable fractures of a shattered connection. Melissa's laughter, a melody now lost to the echoes of remorse, reverberated in the recesses of my mind. Her eyes, once a haven of trust, stared accusingly from the canvas of my memories, a testament to the wounds I had inflicted.

I awoke to a dawn that offered no solace, its muted hues a stark contrast to the vibrant spectrum of emotions that had colored our shared moments. The emptiness enveloped me like a suffocating shroud. With a heavy heart, I rose from the bed, the weight of my actions pressing upon me like an unforgiving burden.

THE NEXT SEVERAL days unfolded with a relentless monotony, a procession of hours that held no meaning in the absence of her presence. The phone lay silent, its silence echoing the void left by her departure. I paced the rooms, haunted by the silence, my footsteps a hollow percussion against the hollowness that enveloped me.

The world outside carried on, oblivious to the tempest that raged within. Birds sang their oblivious melodies, and sunlight filtered through curtains, casting shadows that danced like phantoms of what once was. I stood at the window, a solitary silhouette against the backdrop of a world that had ceased to make sense.

I dialed a number etched into my memory, fingers trembling as I sought a connection that had been severed by my own hand.

The line hummed with anticipation, and when a familiar voice answered, I hesitated for a moment, the words caught in the quagmire of my remorse. "Melissa," I whispered, the syllables carrying the weight of an apology that could never fully bridge the chasm I had created.

The silence that followed broke me.

The connection crackled with a fragile tension, the silence between us echoing like the space between heartbeats. "Melissa," I repeated, the name a plea and an acknowledgment of the fractures I had inflicted upon the symphony of our shared existence. "I'm sorry," the words emerged, hesitant and burdened, but sincere in their intent.

A breath, pregnant with emotions, lingered on the line. In that suspended moment, the weight of my actions hung in the air like the delicate petals of a wilting flower. I could almost hear her thoughts, a tumultuous storm of pain and betrayal. The abyss that had yawned open between us seemed insurmountable, and I braced myself for the silence to stretch into eternity.

Then, a soft exhale, a sound akin to the stirring of winds through a desolate landscape, reached my ears.

"Why?" Her voice, a fragile thread woven with sorrow, held an inquiry that cut through the air like a blade.

The question hung in the balance, a testament to the complexity of human emotions and the intricacies of our entwined destinies. "I thought it would keep you safe," I confessed, the words carrying the burden of a misguided protector, a guardian who had lost sight of the very essence of what he sought to safeguard.

A sigh, laden with the weight of shared history, wafted through the phone. "Safety," she echoed, the syllables lingering between us like the ghosts of promises broken. "You pushed me away for safety?"

The incredulity in her voice shook the foundations of my resolve. The intricacies of my motives unraveled in the face of her disbelief. "I thought I was doing what was best," I muttered, the feeble defense sounding hollow even to my own ears.

There was a pause, a pregnant silence that mirrored the spaces between stars in a vast night sky. "You don't get to decide what's best for me," she declared, her words resonating with a newfound strength. "You don't get to break us apart and then claim it's for my safety."

Her resilience, a beacon in the darkness, illuminated the depth of her wounds. "Melissa, please," I implored, the desperation in my voice bared like a soul laid bare. "I can't undo the past, but I want to make amends. I want to find us again. I miss you."

Another pause, as if the universe itself held its breath, waiting for the threads of fate to weave a new tapestry. "Us," she murmured, the word a whisper wrapped in the echoes of what once was. "There might not be an 'us' left."

A chill gripped my heart, and I clung to the fragile hope that lingered like a flickering candle flame. "I love you," I confessed, the words spilling forth with a vulnerability that stripped away the layers of pretense. "And I understand if you can't forgive me. But I can't walk away without trying."

The line crackled again; the fragile bridge of connection tested by the forces that sought to pull it apart. "Love," she echoed, the syllable heavy with the weight of unspoken truths. "It's not enough."

The admission struck with the force of a thousand shattered dreams. In the aftermath of her words, the echoes of my own inadequacies reverberated. I had underestimated the fragility of what we had, and in my blind pursuit of protection, I had become the very threat I sought to shield her from.

"Goodbye."

As the line fell silent, I stared into the abyss of the unknown. The journey ahead seemed daunting, a path fraught with uncertainty and the haunting shadows of mistakes past. Yet, in that moment of vulnerability, I found a glimmer of determination—a resolve to rebuild what I had dismantled, to navigate the labyrinth of forgiveness, and, perhaps, to discover redemption in the fragments of a love that refused to be extinguished.

A solitary candle flickered on the edge of the table, its wavering flame a dance that mirrored the fragility of hope. I traced the rim of the glass containing the remnants of bourbon, the amber liquid now a reflection of my own internal turmoil. The room, once a sanctuary for shared laughter and whispered confessions, now stood as a testament to the fractures I had carved into the foundation of us.

The phone, a lifeline to a world beyond my solitude, lay still. Melissa's presence lingered in its silence, her absence a void that seemed to expand with every passing moment. I wondered if the abyss between us could ever be bridged, if the scars etched into the tapestry of our love could be mended.

With a sigh, I wandered through the empty corridors of memory. Each room held remnants of our shared existence frozen in moments of joy, the echo of her laughter, the imprint of her touch on the walls of my heart. I moved through the spaces that had once been alive with the warmth of connection, now haunted by the ghostly whispers of what once was.

The residue of bourbon on my lips was a bitter reminder of the choices that had led us to this precipice. Love, once a beacon that illuminated our shared path, now felt like a distant constellation, its brilliance obscured by the clouds of regret. I wondered if love alone could navigate the treacherous terrain of forgiveness.

In the solitude of the night, a decision crystallized within me—an acknowledgment that the journey to redemption would be fraught with challenges, but the pursuit of what remained of us was a quest worth undertaking. With hesitant fingers, I picked up the phone, its cool surface a conduit to the possibility of healing.

I called her number, each digit a deliberate step towards the unknown. The ringing seemed to stretch into eternity, a suspended moment where the fate of our connection hung in the balance. And then, she answered, her voice a fragile melody that danced through the void.

"Melissa, don't' hang up," I began, the syllables laden with a sincerity that surpassed mere words. "I don't expect you to forgive me easily, or perhaps, not at all. But I want you to know that every fiber of my being aches with the knowledge of what I've done."

The admission hung in the air, a confession that laid bare the vulnerability of my soul. The night held its breath, as if awaiting the verdict of a cosmic trial.

Her response, when it came, carried the weight of a thousand unspoken emotions.

"Is love enough?" she asked, her voice a delicate tremor.

The question echoed in the hollows of my chest, demanding a reckoning with the inadequacies of my past actions.

"No, it's not," I replied, the honesty cutting through the layers of pretense. "But it's the foundation on which we can rebuild. I'm willing to navigate the complexities, to earn back the trust I shattered."

The silence that followed was profound, a chasm that seemed to stretch into the core of our shared history. "I need time," she finally said, the words a fragile bridge spanning the expanse between us.

Melissa

It had been three weeks.

Twenty-one days.

Since Billy had told me to go.

He'd been so angry with me during those last moments... the night I'd admitted how I felt, and he'd shoved me away.

I couldn't deny that it hurt.

God, it had fucking hurt like no other.

But I knew he was lying.

I knew the harsh things he'd spat at me were nothing but a ploy. It had worked, but he wasn't fooling anyone, least of all me and himself.

He cared about me, and the fact it was evident he couldn't process those emotions, ones that led him to create havoc all around him, told me all I needed to know.

He was a scary man, but one who cared for me sincerely.

I recall well the way he looked at me, the way he touched me, and the way he whispered words in my ear when he thought I wasn't awake.

I didn't want to ponder that he didn't care for me as profoundly as I cared for him. We were two opposing ends of the spectrum. He wasn't good for me.

That life.

The danger that surrounded him.

All of that was nothing but a fuse waiting to be lit, the detonation of the bomb anticipating an explosion. And if I understood all of this, that he wasn't right for me and I deserved more, needed more, why was I so lonely?

Why did I feel that something was missing from my life?

I locked the front door to my one-bedroom apartment. The city I picked was hours from Desolation. It was clean. It was safe. Or it offered the illusion of protection. I wasn't a fool in thinking that because I was gone from that muck nothing horrible would ever touch me.

I knew how the world worked, how people and men operated in order to get their way.

Some areas were nothing more than a level of hell waiting to burn you alive.

I obtained a job almost immediately after arriving here. I didn't need to work. Not after Billy had given me so much money. I'd never be able to spend it in my lifetime. But until I decided what I wanted to do with my life, I had to keep active.

Because I couldn't stop thinking of him.

A part of me hated that I couldn't stop thinking about Billy. I knew the things he did. I understood what he'd done to reach the top.

But I also knew how kind he could be.

Gentle and protective.

As in... murdering a man in his own home for touching me.

I repeated all those dreadful things in my thoughts, the words that had been uttered and the way he'd looked at me right before I left.

They ate away at me. Yet, I wanted to go back to him, slap him across the face, and tell him to wake the fuck up.

Did he miss me?

Was he thinking about me as much as I was him?

I set my bag on the counter, something heavy hitting the granite. A peek inside showed the large hunting knife sitting at the bottom. Billy had given it to me, or I thought it was him who had slipped it with my belongings before I'd left.

Snowed in with the Mafia

All my shit had been ready and waiting by the front doors, as if he'd been counting down the hours until he could kick me out.

I'd ordered Robert to take me to the bus station. I didn't know where I was going, but I wouldn't have informed Billy's right-hand guy anyway. Not that it mattered. I knew a man like Billy would find me no matter where I was.

I'd taken a bus schedule, closed my eyes, and pointed to a random area.

And that's how I'd come to live in North Point, New York. A three-hour bus trip was a fresh start for me.

I put up the groceries I'd bought on the way home from work and then got ready for the diner. Once clothed, I gazed around my modest apartment.

It was nice. Nicer and cleaner than anything I'd ever lived in, not counting Billy's estate, that was.

The apartment was sleek and stylish. It had come fully furnished, so none of the stuff filling the room was mine. This entire area wasn't even… me.

I felt like a stranger living amongst someone else's possessions. I leaned against the kitchen island and closed my eyes, breathing out. It seemed like another panic episode was welling up, one that came on as suddenly as it passed.

I believed getting out of Desolation would do me good. I'd be a new person. I'd have a new life.

It'd be everything I ever wanted.

But it had taken me no time at all to grasp that you could take the girl out of her gloomy world but couldn't take that darkness out of her. With one more quick look around, I grabbed the keys and my purse and headed back out.

The trip to the diner was only a couple of blocks. I passed a bagel shop. A trendy little smoothie kiosk. There was a small, handcrafted furniture business right down the street that specializes in handmade bowls and kitchenware.

The walkways were constructed of cobblestone. The

lamps are old bronze. I felt so out of fucking place that it made my gut tighten somewhat. There was also a bar on every freaking street corner, the local college kids frequenting them every weekend.

The sun hadn't even fallen, but said bars were already buzzing, the young people barely legal drinking age and already working on becoming shitfaced.

I passed the street and walked another block before I got to work. It was a little fifties retro-style cafe that offered homemade pies and ice cream and was known for their over-the-top milkshakes and sandwiches.

It was a fast shift for me tonight. Just four hours, so I covered the dinner rush.

I was convinced people thought I was a snobbish bitch because I kept to myself. My coworkers barely spoke to me, and I knew it was because I had a resting bitch face firmly in place. It was a defensive mechanism for me.

Not creating connections with other people and remaining invisible was how I'd stayed alive in Desolation.

And it worked. But I'd never make friends being so distant and coming across as standoffish.

Did I really want these people to be part of my life?

They wore polo shirts, penny loafers, and pressed khakis. The men looked like they went golfing on the weekends while their wives drank mimosas and gossiped.

And despite having more money than I could ever count, I still shopped at local thrift stores, bought clearance items off the rack, and looked at sale products at the grocery store.

I didn't think I'd ever transform my thoughts and body, constantly in that survival mode.

For the next four hours, I focused on my job, putting on that artificial smile that would earn a few extra dollars in tip money I didn't actually need.

It was near the end of my shift that I got a dinner to go

discounted with my employee status headed out, and made rapid work returning to my flat.

A hot bath, cool beer with my meal, and maybe even a movie I'd already seen ten times over was how I was planning to spend my night.

It's how I seemed to spend all my nights.

And that was perfect, if I were being honest. Being home and not being terrified was still such a foreign issue, something I hoped I could feel comfortable with one day.

I was adjusting my take-out bag when I rounded the corner and walked by one of the newest bars on the block.

It had an Irish pub feel to it, as if someone had taken every clichéd thing, they assumed an establishment like that possessed and placed it in this location.

I strolled past a group of guys who I could smell before I even passed them. The booze around them was strong enough I wondered whether I could get drunk from the smells alone.

"Hey, pretty girl."

I didn't look at them, didn't even acknowledge their existence. After living in Desolation for my entire life, I understood when to be inconspicuous. Silent.

It was a survival instinct, one that was ingrained in me.

The catcalls continued followed by whistling. They yelled unpleasant and crude things, but compared to what I'd been called, their statements were almost amusing.

I was almost at the end of the block when I heard someone approaching, footfall on pavement quicker as they sought to catch up with me.

Everything in me tightened, and automatically, I reached inside my backpack for the knife that Billy had given me.

The handle was cold and hard in my palm, my hold sturdy. I still recalled the feeling that had possessed me when I opened up my bag and had found it resting there, encased in leather, the blade so keen when I pulled it out, I'd cut myself.

Like a hot knife through butter.

But the boy, because that's exactly what he was, didn't touch me. He moved in front of me and turned, racing backward with a smirk on his face. His forehead was greasy and his hair disheveled. He reeked of drunkenness that not even his overwhelming fragrance could conceal.

"Hey, we were talking to you. Didn't you hear?"

I stayed silent.

He grinned as if amazed I ignored him. "Too good to respond?"

I could hear other footsteps behind me as his pals caught up.

I just kept my concentration on the pavement as I kept walking. A few times, I had to step to the side so I didn't run into him, but he maintained pace with me the entire way, continuing to ask me questions that I refused to answer.

But it was when I was close to my apartment building that I had a feeling he wasn't going to let up. I didn't want him to see where I lived. He was just some drunk college kid who seemed harmless. He made me uneasy, but not in the dangerous way I felt when I was surrounded by lowlifes, my brother and father included.

God, Billy would gobble this little shit up and spit him out till there was nothing but skin and bones scattered on the ground.

I was going to take a different path, hopefully losing him, because it was clearly evident this idiot wasn't giving up or taking the hint.

The two boys behind me plainly were the followers as they weren't even paying attention to me. Instead, they talked to each other about their college classes.

But as the moron reached out and tried to touch my hair, the girl who'd survived a shitload of stuff, who'd been slapped too many times by her father and brother, rose.

The girl who had to battle tooth and nail just to keep above water when it felt like a tsunami was covering her came up like a warrior poised to destroy everything around her.

He grabbed on my hair, and I swung around, brandishing that knife and holding it up between us, the blade pointed at the fucker. My hand was steady, eyes narrowed, and vision focused.

His astonished expression came on instantaneously, but that soon faded to rage.

Oh, he was one of those.

His buddies, who chuckled, broke that astonished moment of quiet. "Holy fucking shit," one of them exclaimed.

"This fucking bitch pulled out a damn gutting knife, man."

I paid them no heed. They weren't the ones who were threatening me at this moment. Maybe this douchebag wasn't a true threat, but it wasn't a risk I would accept.

"What exactly are you going to do?" the fucker seethed.

I still stayed silent.

He took a step forward, and on reflex, I swiped out, the blade nicking his forearm. He growled out a curse and held his arm back, looking down at the small, very clear, superficial cut. A bit of blood welled up before trickling down his forearm to drip off his elbow.

"Bitch, do you know who I am? Pulling a knife on me is going to get your life destroyed." He took a step closer but paused when I did the same, the tip of the blade pushing into his chest.

"I've dealt with real dangerous men. Unlike you." It was the first time I'd said anything. "Killing won't be something new for me, asshole."

After a long while, he pursed his lips, moved back, and held his hands up.

His companions had since shut talking, maybe detecting this crazy energy in me. I felt unhinged. This wasn't a usual reaction for me. But ever since my time with Billy and now weeks later being alone and feeling more lost than I ever had in my life made me not act like myself.

Fuck this guy.

He was so fortunate and probably got everything he wanted. The entitled prick had screwed with the wrong women.

"Leave me alone," was all I murmured.

We were in a stalemate for several moments until he took another step back and then another.

"Big fucking mistake."

Then he turned and departed, his friends following.

I didn't move, keeping my eyes on him the entire time. It was only after they went around the corner that I slowly lowered the knife and exhaled. A rush of adrenaline raced through my veins, and I breathed out again, feeling more cantered with each passing second.

God, why did I ever assume that simply because I left Desolation my life would be easier?

Safer?

Being fully honest and upfront with myself, moving away made things feel a lot harder than they ever had been.

A lot scarier.

Definitely lonelier.

I arrived back at my apartment, shut the door, triple checked it, and kept the knife in my hand. I ran the bath, grabbed a cool beer, my supper and tablet, and for the next hour and a half disconnected.

But my uneasiness never waned.

In fact, I felt it growing stronger with each passing moment.

Melissa

I WASN'T sure what had woken me, but it seemed like ants were moving over my skin. I scratched my arms and sat up in bed, gazing around.

After completing three beers, I'd climbed out of the icy bath, fell into bed, and contentedly let the beer carry me to sleep.

It was still dark, the subdued glimmer of the streetlight across from my apartment building sending a sliver of lamp through the split in the drapes. The clock on the nightstand said it was just three in the morning.

An idle thought that he'd come for me went through my thoughts. But it had been weeks since I had left Billy, and he hadn't reached out to me.

I felt like I was being watched multiple times but passed it off to my new surroundings. There always appeared to be a tingle on the back of my neck whenever I walked out of my apartment.

I lay back down and stared at the ceiling, observing as the headlights from passing cars occasionally moved across the room. But I couldn't ignore the feeling that something just wasn't right. I reached beneath the pillow, the knife nestled snugly underneath my head, and curled my hand around the handle.

After ten minutes of not being able to fall back asleep, I

got out of bed, threw on an oversized hoodie, and grabbed the knife to take with me into the kitchen.

I stood by the sink and sipped a glass of water, the small clock that hung on the wall counting down the seconds.

I peered out the kitchen window and felt that tingle on the back of my neck again, that tightening on my arms. And then I heard movement, maybe scratching, down in the alley directly below the window.

Investigating what created that noise was something only a fool would do, the kind of person who was the first to die in a horror movie.

Fuck that.

Not me.

I took my knife, went back to bed, and didn't sleep the rest of the night while I stared at the ceiling because I knew I wasn't alone.

Melissa

THE NEXT WEEK, I was in a fog, in a daze of going to work and coming back home. I didn't go anywhere aside from places like the grocery store or laundry mat.

Instead, I shut myself away like a hermit.

I'd established a self-imposed jail.

It was a monotonous life, and the longer it went on, the more I loathed it. The last month had made me feel as if I were living in someone else's life, walking in their shoes, stuck within them, and able to see everything. And through it all, I couldn't react.

It was a Saturday night when I clocked out and headed home, my handbag slung over my shoulder, my hand in the bag. Although I still had the knife with me, I also carried pepper spray, my finger clamped over the nozzle just in case and always at the ready.

Nobody really troubled me, not aside from that one college jackass. But I hadn't seen him since. I'd stayed away from the pub following that incident, but being cautious meant little.

The streets were crowded for the weekend, college youngsters walking around, elderly people enjoying their drinks on the outside patios at the little, elegant bars.

I glanced at the street to see automobiles passing. A dark SUV with tinted-out windows attracted my attention. There wasn't anything spectacular about it. It appeared like any other vehicle that I saw. But while I stared at it, I felt this peculiar tingle in the pit of my belly.

My mind quickly went to Billy. I wanted so desperately to think it was him.

Foolish, silly girl.

Wanting to play with fire even though I knew I'd get burned was obviously a new trend with me.

I rounded the curve and glanced over my shoulder at that SUV once more. I swore I felt the driver observing me even if I couldn't see through the dark windows.

When I faced ahead once more, I ran into somebody so hard I stumbled back and had to support a hand on the building alongside me. He cursed out a juicy and dirty insult.

"The fuck. Watch where you're going." His voice was deep and raspy, a little lazy because it was clear he'd been drinking.

I simply gave him one short look before murmuring a sorry and continuing to go.

Fuck this.

I was going to move to the mountains. I'd find a tiny hut in the middle of nowhere. If I was going to feel alone amongst masses of people, I might as well feel the same way by myself without these fuckers invading my space.

Go to Billy. Demand he be honest with himself and you.

I was making a change tomorrow.

Fuck this place.

I'd pack up my luggage, head to the bus station, and pick a city far away. And when I got there, I'd do the same thing. I wouldn't stop until I was in the middle of nowhere.

Coming up on my building, I was abruptly pushed from behind. I faltered and went to my knees, my hands landing hard on the ground, the heels of my palms getting scraped up.

"Oh shit," the drunken, male voice murmured from behind me.

I was about to lift myself up, but his hands on my waist drove the action so I had no choice but to do it.

"I'm sorry." He laughed.

I forced myself away from him, staring down at my skinned hands, and snarled out when I felt the burn of them when I ran them down my jeans.

"It's fine." I began to go when he grabbed my arm.

"Hey."

His grasp tightened on my wrist, and I grimaced.

"Let go."

I pulled my arm, but his hold was like a vise.

He let go but continued forward so I was obliged to step back. I saw we were now in the side alley in between a closed bakery and car dealership.

"I think I've seen you before." He was smirking, all sweaty and stinking like beer. "Yeah." He pointed to me, his smile broadening. "You work down the street. At that fifty's diner, yeah?"

"I have to go." I started to move past him but he pushed forward, pressing me so I moved back again, the brick of the wall pushing me to stay in place.

Something shifted in his demeanor the longer he stared at me.

Heart thumping hard in my chest, I kept my concentration on him as I reached in my purse and curled my palm around the first object I felt. The knife. My flight-or-fight instinct kicked into gear. But more importantly... my strength rose.

"I bet you smell good." He leaned nearer. "I bet you feel even better between those long legs." He shoved his body against me, his erection firm and frightening.

Fuck.

No.

"Come on," he muttered, his hot breath in my face. "We're alone. I'll be speedy. It'll be over before you even know it." He reached down to pull himself out of his jeans, but I didn't let him get that far.

I had the knife out, but he noticed it and curled his lip, lashing out with his fist. His knuckle caught my chin, but he was too inebriated that it barely skimmed me. I knew if he got the opportunity, he would knock me the hell out.

I swung out, but I didn't know if I'd connected. It was only when I felt the spray of blood covering my face and neck that my breath caught in my chest, and I was frozen in place.

I felt those droplets pouring down my cheeks and chin, that silky fluid slowly turning sticky as it enveloped my fingers and wrists.

I felt my eyes widen in amazement at the enormous cut on the side of his throat. He placed his hand on the side of his neck, his mouth opened in horror when he lifted his fingers to his face to see blood covering them.

For what seemed like minutes, we just stood there, staring at each other.

I'd never injured a man like this.

I'd never killed a man before.

"You stupid fucking bitch."

Although I knew that wound had to be life-threatening because of the amount of blood that came out, it was like a strength coursed through him as he narrowed his eyes, bared his teeth, and lunged at me.

I threw my arm out, the handle slippery in my palm from the blood. I anticipated him to slam into me and take me to the ground, but that never happened. Somebody rushed out from the shadows and dragged the person back, flinging him away, as if he were a rag doll. His body landed with a hard bang on the pavement.

He scarcely had half a second to understand what was happening before the big figure was grabbing the knife from my grasp, kneeling next to the asshole, and opening his neck from ear to ear.

Oh. God.

Even in the gloomy alleyway, I saw his flesh open up,

dividing so readily. Blood spurted out, throbbing with each beat of his heart.

Billy was here.

He'd come for me.

After a long second, Billy stood menacingly over the dead guy. The weak light from the streetlamp showered him in a mellow yellow tint. I felt my eyes expand as Billy gently turned to face me. He brushed his palms over his suit, his hands looking dark like spilled ink covered them.

I grew dizzy. My legs threatened to give out from under me, but Billy was by me a second later.

He brought my body close to his, his stare fixated on the side of my jaw where I'd been punched.

"I wanted to kill that motherfucker for even looking in your direction." He kissed my forehead, then my cheeks, and then gave me the lightest brush of his lips to my jawline.

Billy started walking me out of the alley, and I lifted my chin up, refusing to act weak and defenseless. I attempted to push him away and move on my own, but his deep chuckle and the way he kissed the top of my forehead had me leaning against him.

Billy

"Where are you taking me?" she asked in a hazy voice.

My girl wasn't a stranger to violence or death, and she was tough as hell.

I admired her.

But I noticed how she kept glancing at her hands, seeing the drying blood coating them.

She was still so pure even after living in the filth that was Desolation.

"I'm taking you home, Sunshine." I put my arm snugly around her waist and walked her to the SUV parked across the street. I was glad she wasn't fighting me for being the stronger one right now.

She'd done well, my darling girl.

That fucker would have died from the cut in his neck, but I'd finished the job. I didn't want that on her hands, and truth be told, I wanted to fucking kill him ten times over just for breathing in her direction.

I'd phone Robert and have some of our associates take care of the body before anyone could locate it. I opened the rear door, picked Melissa up, and laid her in the back. She didn't fight me, and as I covered her with my jacket, she curled into a ball so she appeared even smaller.

Something painful clenched in my heart at seeing her so tired, so terrified, almost defeated in a way I hadn't witnessed before.

"Let's go home, sweetheart."

I leaned in and kissed her temple, cupping the back of her head and held her close for long seconds, simply feeling her.

Smelling her.

"I'm never letting you fucking go. I'll kill any motherfucker who stands in my way of making that my reality."

With one more kiss to her head, I climbed in the driver's seat and headed home.

Home.

That's what it felt like with Melissa as mine.

Billy

It had taken us hours to get back to my apartment. That's how far she had moved away from me.

As soon as we arrived, I had the staff make her something hot to drink and eat, and I started a bath for her. Slowly, as she soaked, she started to relax until she laid back with a towel tucked behind her neck and her eyes closed as I bathed her.

She didn't fight me as I rubbed the washcloth over her nude body, and I didn't know if that should alarm me because she was in shock or if I should be pleased because it indicated she was completely mine and felt comfortable with me.

"What are you thinking, Mellie?"

She didn't answer immediately, but I didn't press her to respond. I wanted her to feel safe and comfortable with me. I felt different with her.

At peace.

When she wasn't around, I was the dark man who did whatever he had to in order to survive.

But with Melissa?

I felt this warmth consume me.

And I had missed it.

I wanted it forever.

"You killed a man for no reason."

I felt my whole demeanor darken at her words. "No reason? He spoke to you. That's enough of a cause to kill him.

If I'd had more time, I would have chopped off his dick and forced it down his throat."

She opened her eyes, her throat straining as she swallowed after I whispered those words.

"I killed your worthless brother and father because they hurt you." I brushed a finger over her cheek. "I killed that prick from the week before who you drew your knife on."

She cleared her throat, her expression revealing she was astonished I knew about that. "You were following me this whole time?" She changed the subject, and I let her.

Or maybe she didn't.

Maybe she needed clarity on what I'd done.

I wanted to express in great detail all the things I would have done to that guy to make sure she realized how much I could, and would, protect her.

The sound of the water flowing into the tub as I lifted the washcloth and ran it over her neck was the only sound around us.

"Yes," was all I murmured, but when she opened her eyes and let her head fall slightly to the side so she could look at me, I continued. "I told myself not to. I convinced myself pushing you away and letting you go was what I had to do. But I lasted one fucking day, Sunshine."

She inhaled deeply but exhibited no emotion at what I said.

"Last week I gutted the fucker who touched you. His father was a lawmaker. He attempted pleading for his life with the information. I made his dying slower because of it."

"I won't even ask how you knew where I was," she murmured.

I smirked and ran the towel over her arm. "I would find you no matter where you ran off to, pretty girl." I let the cloth fall into the tub and braced my forearms on the edge of the porcelain, just staring into her eyes.

"I was hoping you'd come for me."

My heart constricted tightly in my chest after hearing those words utter from Melissa's sweet lips. I reached out and brushed my thumb over her cheek, over her jawline, and over the pad of her bottom lip, tugging the flesh down and letting it snap back into place.

"I hated that I felt that way but never wanted it to go away."

God, what this chick did to me was like an electrical bolt right to my chest.

"I've never wanted anything as much as I want you." I leaned in, my mouth close to hers. "I've been watching you from the moment you moved into that apartment. I watched you as you worked and made sure you arrived home okay, every night."

Something flared in her eyes, and I slowly grinned. "I made sure that motherfucker who touched you got his hand broken."

She shifted in the tub, the water sloshing as she grew conscious.

"I didn't kill him, even though I really fucking wanted to." I moved in and grasped her chin, bringing my mouth to hers as I kissed her hard. "But I made sure I hurt him. Real fucking bad, Mellie. I made that asshole cry for his papa. I won't make the mistake of letting you go again. You're mine."

I pressed my mouth to hers and bit her lip, causing her to gasp and pull back. But with my hand clasped tightly around her nape, I kept her close to my face.

"Say you're mine."

I felt violent with my feelings.

She was quiet too long, so I said it harder.

"Say you're fucking mine, Melissa."

She sat up, facing me completely and took on a steely glare. It was sweet and amusing how serious she appeared. "I planned on running off and living in the middle of the woods. Being alone for the rest of my life felt like an acceptable alternative to missing you like crazy and wishing I was with you."

I let out a deep growl, one that came from all the built-up possessiveness. I was about to demand she tell me that she was mine when she cupped my face, silencing me with gentleness.

She looked me in the eyes and stated in the nicest fucking voice, "I'm yours, and you're mine. Don't forget it."

I grinned, feeling like a ton of fucking bricks had just been lifted off my chest. I hauled her out of the tub not giving a shit that she was totally wet and my clothing was ruined.

They'd be coming off regardless.

I took her to bed where I fucked my gorgeous lady three times and called her my whore before I allowed her go to sleep.

Melissa

EVEN A YEAR LATER, I wanted to cuss him out, to tell Billy to fuck off. But the reality was, the only reason such ideas even crossed my mind was because we both got off on me playing hard to get.

And I wasn't about to deny either of us right now.

When I didn't listen immediately away, Billy made a disapproving sound and stepped closer till he surrounded me, until his enormous body was nearly crushed right to mine.

I retained my cool and tried to appear like my pussy wasn't moist for this very dangerous man whom I loved more than anything else.

"You'll learn soon enough to do as I say, pretty girl." His concentration went to my mouth, his eyes getting hooded. "You always look so gorgeous with your mouth all red and swollen from sucking my dick."

Billy rubbed the pad of his thumb over my lower lip, the sensation rough, demanding. "So damn pretty." He tugged the flesh down, a hard groan from him. "Never seen anything so fucking hot before."

I sighed and closed my eyes, my veneer of disinterest unraveling.

"There she is," he muttered. "Be a good girl and don't make me tell you again."

I opened my eyes to see him stroking himself. His motions

were unhurried, as if he had all the time in the world to degrade and praise me.

"Sink down on those knees and come closer, Sunshine."

My body was on fire, blazing from the inside out, making me feel like I'd burn this entire room down. I was already naked, having responded promptly when he commanded me to strip.

And so, I got to my knees and looked up at him. "Closer, sweet girl."

The floor was rough and chilly yet it did wicked things where my arousal was concerned.

"Don't make me ask you again, Melissa."

Billy's voice was rough, like he'd been drinking whiskey all night.

I crawled nearer him, and with each inch I moved, the more my body lighted up.

This was so degrading... so arousing.

This was the very good type of wrong.

He kept retreating back the closer I came, that handsome bastard. When I was kneeling straight before him, he stretched out and tipped my chin back, so it forced me to stare into his devilishly handsome and brutal face.

For several seconds, he did nothing but look at me, his thumb stroking my jawline, his nostrils flaring every time he inhaled hard.

"Do you understand how much I love you?"

My heart skipped a beat when his own mask of indifference and apathy slipped, and I saw the man who showed me a new side that no one else had witnessed.

I nodded. "I love you, too."

He shook his head. "Not like me. Never like me." He inhaled deeply. "I'd scorch the fucking world for you to prove my love. I'd slit my wrists and let you drink my blood till my heart died if it meant you lived on."

I didn't know what to say. No words were suitable for what

he just declared. I knew his comments were the real truth, and even if I told him I felt the same, it would never sink in. He would never imagine I could love him as deeply as he confessed to loving me.

So, I showed him with my body what he meant to me.

With one more delicate stroke to my chin, he let go of me and clutched that big cock dangling between his knees once more, his mask back in place.

He was hard, but God, the more he stroked himself, the thicker and longer he became.

I felt like a deviant as my mouth watered shamelessly. I was in this hazy reality as I glanced at Billy and knew what was about to happen.

"Sweet girl," he purred like the devil. "You know you want to please me." The way he jerked himself off from root to tip and the sight of droplets of transparent pre-cum dotting the crown had me feeling like a wildfire coursed within me.

I was so drenched.

My inner muscles tensed, my clit throbbed, and the sloppy feeling of the mess I was generating between my thighs because I was so excited should have humiliated me.

"How much do you want to suck my cock?"

I shivered and moaned. "God… so much." I didn't know when I lifted my hands or when I placed them on his thighs, but I brushed my palms over his jeans. He'd simply taken his cock out through the fly, so he was still completely dressed.

I found it insanely hot.

"That's my good, dirty little girl."

I glanced up at him as I curled my fingers on his thighs, pressing my nails into his flesh and wanting him to hurt as much as he did to me… in the best way.

"Look at it," he commanded in a low, harsh voice.

I lowered my concentration to stare at his erection, the length thick, the skin stretched tight since he was so hard.

I stroked my hands over his thighs, his jeans rough under

my palms. I was about to grip his cock when my fingertips skated over something square and hard protruding beneath his jeans pocket.

I felt his body tense under my contact when I looked up at him, my fingers still on that rigid item.

My heart thundered because I knew.

I just knew what it was without ever seeing it.

His gaze had me whispering his name.

"Fuck," he murmured quietly with zero heat behind that lone curse word.

A second later, he got his hands under my arms and lifted me from the ground. He embraced me, his palm cupping the back of my head, his nose pressed to the side of my throat as he inhaled deeply.

"I was going to wait until we were in the air."

His statements bewildered me, but he didn't make me wait to examine what he meant.

"The normal proper way to do this would be to drop on one knee…"

"That's not you," I answered, cutting him off.

His deep chuckle vibrated my neck, and he tightened his palm in my hair.

"No, it's not, Sunshine." He breathed. "But I want to be that man for you."

"I don't want you to be anyone you're not. I adore you the way you are." His entire body went ramrod tight against me; his fingers painful in my hair as he pulled me impossibly closer.

"Say it again."

I closed my eyes and rested my head in the center of his chest. "I love you."

"Again."

I smiled to myself. "I love you, Billy. Maybe I shouldn't since it's not like you're the hero."

"I'm the fucking villain, and you love that."

"Mmm, I sure do."

And I did.

It was bizarre and wondrous, terrifying and exhilarating.

But I loved the bad guy.

My bad guy.

He pulled back and placed his hand possessively around my throat. For a prolonged while, he didn't speak, his black eyes burning holes into me as if he were thinking hard on what he would say next.

"You'll marry me." It wasn't a question. "You'll be mine. Only mine." It sounded like he snarled that last part, and every feminine part of me tingled in response.

"Is that so?" I cocked an eyebrow, knowing I was playing with fire. "Melissa," he growled my name, and my toes curled.

"Yes, Billy."

His steely countenance suddenly turned into a softer one he exclusively saved for me.

"I'm already yours, but if you want to put that ring in your pocket on my finger to make it official…" I rose on my toes and kissed him. "Then so be it. So, yes." I wrapped my arms around his shoulders, and he lifted me so the tips of my toes barely touched the floor. "I'll be your wife."

He placed his forehead against mine, but after barely a second of that, set me back on the floor, removed the box from his pocket, and showed me the biggest, most exquisite piece of jewelry I'd ever seen.

Just like Billy, the ring was simplistic but complicated. The band featured filigree work, and the diamond, a square-cut solitaire as big as my damn eye, glittered back.

"I wanted bigger but your hands and fingers are so tiny."

I giggled gently as he put the ring, so heavy into my finger.

"Now, say it again." His voice was gruff, and I wondered whether it was because he was filled with so much emotion.

I didn't need him to elaborate. I knew what he wanted because it was the same as what I did. "I'm yours, Billy." I adopted a stern face, one he gave me so many times, yet the twitch of his lips told me he thought it hilarious, not threatening.

"My sweet girl." He kissed the tip of my nose. "I'm yours, Melissa. I have been since the minute I saw you."

We kissed and kissed and kissed till my lips felt damaged and I was breathless.

"Now suck my dick like Daddy's good girl, and I'll reward you by shooting my load down your throat."

A moan was ripped from me. That wonderful moment we'd just experienced was snatched away in the face of our ongoing need for one another.

"Then I'm taking my girl to Italy, marrying you, and letting every fucking jealous bastard know you're mine."

I grinned softly, went to my knees, and swallowed my future husband's dick until his eyes rolled back and he came down my throat.

Join Maya Black's Newsletter

Thank you for reading *Snowed in with the Mafia!* If you enjoyed it, I'd appreciate you leaving a review anywhere you can!

If you'd like to join my newsletter you can do so at https://www.subscribepage.com/p3j3r1

What do you get? Inside peeks at covers, help choosing characters, what I'm working on next, and so many more fun items!

See you there!

About Maya Black

Maya Black lives in the Rocky Mountains with her husband and animals and loves being out in nature. She loves all things coffee and books!

She's a new author but has been an avid reader her whole life with stories brewing in her mind. She's finally putting pen to paper to write in a mix of genres but all will include an element of romance.

Join me everywhere you can at https://linktr.ee/authormayablack

Also by Maya Black

ANTHOLOGIES

- Cracked Fairy Tales
- Practical Potions
- Twisted Fairy Tales
- Echoes of the Dead
- Rose of Disgrace - Coming December 2024
- Evil Hearts - Coming February 2025

STANDALONES

- What Might Have Been
- Yule Spice
- Unchained Melody
- Alice's Illusions
- Wishful Witch
- Bet on Love - Coming April 2025

SNOWED IN SERIES

Can be read in any order

- Snowed in with the Mafia
- Snowed in with the Billionaire - Coming January 2025
- Snowed in with the Brother's Best Friend - Coming February 2025
- More coming in Winter 2025/2026